AGE GAP ROMANCE
Part Two

ALSO BY HP MALLORY:

PARANOMAL WOMEN'S FICTION:
Haven Hollow
Misty Hollow
Trailer Park Vampire
Midlife Spirits

PARANORMAL ROMANCE:
Witch & Warlock
Vampire Esquire
Ever Dark Academy

FANTASY ROMANCE:
Dark Destinies
Gates of the Underworld
Lily Harper
Dulcie O'Neil

PARANORMAL REVERSE HAREM:
My Five Kings
Happily Never After

CONTEMPORARY ROMANCE:
Age Gap Romance

SCI-FI ROMANCE:
The Alaskan Detective

TRILOGIES:
Crown of Lies
Dragon's Birthright
Midlife Mermaid
The Dark Circus

Chasing Demons
Dungeon Raider
Here to There
Arctic Wolves
Wolves of Valhalla
Lucy Westenra

AGE GAP ROMANCE
Part Two

Sexy Contemporary Romances
Book # 2

H.P. Mallory

AGE GAP ROMANCE, PART TWO

HP MALLORY

Copyright ©2023 by HP Mallory

All rights reserved. No part of this book may be used or reproduced in any manner whatsoever without written permission, except in the case of brief quotations embodied in critical articles or reviews. Please do not participate in or encourage the piracy of copyrighted materials in violation of the author's rights. Purchase only authorized editions.

ONE
The Femme Fatale Handbook
Chapter Seven: Be Feminine and Make Him Feel Like a Man

Contrary to what you might think, men are actually starved for appreciation, acceptance and admiration.

Understanding that, the best thing you can be is curious. Ask him questions. Be interested in his ideas, his goals, his dreams, his perspectives. Laugh at his jokes and strive to better understand what makes him tick. When you do all these things, you create desire within him. You allow him to see himself reflected in your eyes—yes, it's very narcissistic, but it's also a fact that the seductress understands extremely well. When Cleopatra seduced Antony and Caesar, she did so by making each of them believe he was capable of amazing things. She appealed to each man's inner desire to see himself as great and successful.

One very important point I want to make is that men are attracted to feminine women. If you think of all the examples of seductresses we've seen so far in this handbook, none of them are masculine. Each one uses her femininity to her advantage because she realizes the immense power a woman possesses. In general, women aren't attracted to men that act like women, so why expect men to be attracted to women who act like men?

So, now that you know the importance of using your femininity, just what does that look like? Well, let's go back to the definition of seduction. Ultimately, it's the idea that another person can imagine being sexual with you. That's pretty much it. If you can get him to imagine being sexual with you, or get him to want to be sexual with you, you're essentially seducing him! Things to help get him to think of you in a sexual way:

1. Show some skin. When a man sees a woman he's attracted to, he wants to see her naked. So, the more skin you can comfortably show off, the more you're going to mess with his head. No matter how much or how little of yourself you do show, the key here is that you feel comfortable *in what you're wearing.*

2. Don't be afraid to touch him. Any femme fatale knows that touching a man during a conversation is a very seductive move. Touch his hand, his arm, his chest, etcetera. Just make sure doing so feels natural. Nothing should ever feel or appear to be forced or that will shatter the image you're trying to portray.

3. Play up your best features. In order to be the best version of yourself you can be, make sure you play up your best features with hair, makeup and clothing.

4. Your voice is your ally. Think siren here. Try to sound relaxed, smooth and sweet. Try to stay away from shrill and loud or hurried.

5. Show sexual interest through your gestures, facial expressions and body language—What do I mean by this? Doing little things like biting your lower lip, touching your hair, arching your head back to expose your neck. All little tricks of the trade that women deal in—that trade being slipping a lead around a man's neck so you can have him at your beck and call.

###

DEREK

Nikki was right on time, just like I'd known she would be.

During the time I'd been subbing for the *Feminism in Literature* class, she was late only once. Yes, Nikki was definitely one of those high-achievers I used to laugh at when I was an undergraduate. Back in the day, I would never have imagined that I'd end up in academia. Chasing skirts and getting drunk had appealed to me much more than being scholarly.

Well, if I was going to be honest with myself, I had to admit that I hadn't really changed *that* much. Women were still a favorite pastime of mine, even if the woman who interested me now wasn't one I had any business being interested in. Actually, that shouldn't have surprised me, because I've always been the type of person who wanted what I wasn't supposed to have. And I wasn't supposed to want an undergraduate student.

It was a coldish day so Nikki was dressed somewhat 'conservatively' in tight jeans, high black boots and a skin-tight black turtleneck that did little to hide her impressive bust. Yes, she still looked sexy as hell, but I was relieved that her cleavage wasn't on display and neither were her legs. It just made looking at and talking to her a little easier when I didn't have to control my roving eyes. My roving *mind*, on the other hand, was something I had little hope of controlling, and it was already in the process of imagining Nikki on her knees with my dick in her mouth …

"Nikki," I said to her in greeting as I opened my door and welcomed her into my crowded but small office.

"Hi." She offered me a little smile and took the chair across from my desk. She was holding a brand-new notebook and placed it on the desktop as she fished inside her backpack, pulling out a pen. She opened the notebook and then faced me expectantly.

"You're going to take notes?" I asked with a laugh, unable to conceal my amusement. I closed the door behind me and started for my desk. "You really are a nerd and then some."

"Thanks for that." She frowned up at me. "And last I checked, I didn't have the benefit of a photographic memory, so anything you tell me about being your teaching assistant that's important needs to be written down." Then she paused. "Well, that is if you have anything important to tell me, which is debatable …"

I laughed.

I liked this casual acquaintanceship we now both shared. I hadn't been lying when I'd told her I appreciated the fact that she wasn't afraid of me. It was rare for an undergraduate not to feel some level of submissiveness towards a professor. It was refreshing that such wasn't the case here. Clearly, Nikki was comfortable and confident in her own intelligence and independence, two things that would serve her well in her career life as well as with me.

"Only important things come out of this mouth," I responded with a chuckle.

"Well, that's arguable, but in the interest of time, I'll let it go." She glanced around the room, immediately scrunching up her nose.

"What?"

It wasn't lost on me that I couldn't take my eyes off her. Yes, she was very attractive, there was no arguing that, but it wasn't just her physical beauty that impressed me. It was more her easy and cool confidence—her ability to challenge me. It wasn't as though my obvious attraction to her was going to pose any sort of a problem though, as regarded our working relationship. In general, I tended to find myself surrounded by very attractive women, and I'd always been good at divorcing my dick brain from my intellectual brain.

"Um, someone needs to do some spring, er... *summer* cleaning in here," she answered as she brought her blue eyes to mine and frowned. "I don't know how you can even concentrate with all this crap everywhere."

I looked around the place and nodded with a

sigh. "Yes, well, I'm not that concerned with the state of my office." Then I cleared my throat. "Let's talk about more important subjects."

"Such as?" She poised her pen on her paper and then faced me expectantly.

"Summer session starts in two weeks. If it's just as well with you, I'd like to take those two weeks to get you up to speed with each of the classes so you're familiar with what it is I'll be teaching." Then I shrugged. "Well, the truth of it is that *both* of us will be getting up to speed with Sonama's classes because I can't say I know a damned thing about either one of them."

I'd recently been tasked by the dean to take over Sonama Greco's classes because she'd been badly injured in a car accident and wouldn't be able to teach said classes for some time. I'd been okay with taking over, with the exception of her summer classes because I'd been planning a trip to Thailand. Once the dean had promised me my own T.A., though, I'd reconsidered. And once I'd decided that T.A. should be Nikki, Thailand didn't seem as big a loss as it previously had.

She nodded. "Which classes?"

"Before I answer that question, I should probably inform you that I opted to have you assist me only with general classes rather than the core ones," I started as she glanced up at me quizzically.

"Why's that?"

I shrugged. "I figured we both might get some flak from students who happen to be your peers or older. By focusing on general courses, I thought we might avoid any potentially cumbersome situations, because those classes tend to draw in the freshmen and sophomores. Otherwise, it might be a bit of a conflict of interest since you're also studying for your bachelor's degree. And, of course, you won't be able to take any of my classes moving forward."

She nodded. "That makes sense, and I'm pretty much done with all of my literature core classes anyway, so it's basically a non-issue."

"Good."

She faced me, a question suddenly burning in her eyes. "So, how did you even get this to fly, anyway?"

"Get what part to fly?"

"Me being your assistant. I've never heard of an undergraduate being an assistant to a professor before. I always thought you had to be a graduate student."

"Well, yes, that's been the norm up until now, I guess," I answered with a shrug. "But, the first thing you should know about me is that I tend to get what I want." I gave her a smug smile that I knew would elicit an irritated response.

"Really, Derek?" She frowned at me. "I think I just threw up a little in my mouth."

"Well, I'm sort of kidding," I laughed as I leaned forward, grabbed my stress ball and started kneading it.

"Be serious. How did you get it to fly?"

I cocked my head to the side as I faced her. "Actually, the dean didn't give me *that* hard of a time about it." That was because I'd told him there were only two candidates for the position— Rebecca and Nikki. Of course, I knew there was no way he'd want Rebecca to be my assistant when he wanted her assistance in other ways. Truth be told, there was only one candidate as far as I was concerned, and that candidate was Nikki. There was no way in hell I'd consider Rebecca for the position since she was a psycho bitch, but the dean didn't need to know that. I'd further sweetened the pot by letting it be known that Nikki would work pro-bono so the school's wallet wouldn't be impacted. And that, I believe, had sealed the deal.

"The dean liked the fact that he wouldn't have to pay you," I settled on.

"Hmm, so I guess the rumors aren't true then." She studied me with a curious expression and bobbed the end of her pen against her lips.

"Which rumors?" Most of rumors about me were true, if sometimes a bit exaggerated.

"That you don't get along with the dean," she answered, eyeing me in that way of hers that made it look like she could see right through me. Even though she was only twenty-one, there was something about Nikki that made her seem much older. The more I pondered that fact, the more I realized that she was probably the only woman in my circle who didn't seem ... impressed with me. It was like all my charm was completely lost on her.

Well, you haven't exactly tried to charm her, either, I reminded myself. *If you actually attempted to get her into bed, she'd probably fold just like all the others have. Not that you're going to attempt it, because you aren't ...*

"I wouldn't say it's not true," I answered with a shrug. "I just made it very difficult for him to refuse."

"Okay, well, that's good news then, I guess," she said with her eyebrows arched. "So which classes will I be assisting you with?"

"Number one: *Introduction to Gender, Sexuality and Feminism in American Fiction,*" I started with a frown as I flipped up my index finger. "Two: *Shakespeare's Poetry*, and three: *Lesbian, Gay, Bisexual and Transgender Identities.*" I took a deep breath. "Can you guess which classes are Sonama's and which is mine?"

Nikki threw her head back and laughed so hard, her entire body bounced, including those breasts that were just screaming at me to rip off her sweater.

Down, old boy, down.

Jesus, but this partnership of ours was going to be exhausting if I had to constantly war with my libido.

"The last one doesn't even sound like it's an English Lit class?" she asked.

"Who the hell knows what it is. I have a feeling I'm going to be way out of my comfort zone."

"I think it will be good for you." She nodded and gave me that knowing smile of hers that did nothing but make me want to kiss it right off her lips. "And I've already taken *Shakespeare's Poetry*, so that should make things easier."

"Who taught it?"

"Professor Smith."

I made a face. "That old goat is such a bore! You'll find that I'm much more interesting."

She cocked an amused eyebrow in my direction. "And much humbler, too."

"An attribute I freely admit does not characterize me," I finished with a laugh. And she laughed and then the laughter quieted and we were both left just looking at each other for a few seconds.

"Why do I have the feeling that I'm going to regret taking you up on this offer?" she asked finally, frowning.

"You won't regret it." I dropped my stress ball

and leaned back into my chair.

"I'm not so sure about that."

I chuckled. "Well, let's just say, you're not going to regret it nearly as much as I regret foregoing Thailand in order to teach *Transgender Identity*."

TWO
NIKKI

"Get the chocolate and the powdered ones," Dani said as I parked right outside the door of the nearest twenty-four-hour store.

"You're going to wait here?" I asked when she didn't unbuckle her seat belt.

"Yeah, is that okay?"

"I guess so."

We were on a mission to pick up donuts. In the midst of studying *The Femme Fatale Handbook*,

Dani and I were experiencing a bout of low blood sugar which was compromising our ability to focus. And the answer to an inability to study due to low energy? Donuts. I scooped up two boxes full, paid for them and was on my way out, when I nearly walked headfirst into … Beau, otherwise known as Shit Stain the second.

"Shit," I said in shock, mostly because I nearly found myself up close and personal with his chest.

"I'm glad to see you too," he smirked down at me.

I glanced over at Dani, who was looking down at something, probably her phone, and obviously had no idea who I'd just had the misfortune of nearly colliding with. Reminding myself that Beau had just said something to me, I was about to respond with a snide comment, but then Jane's voice piped up in my head, reminding me to keep my cool. Femme fatales didn't say snide comments—instead they acted cool, calm and collected like nothing could throw them off their game. Luckily, Beau spared me the opportunity to say anything.

"Donuts," he started as he glanced down at the boxes in my hands and his grin broadened. "Please tell me you're bringing those to my house?"

Even though his comment irritated the shit out of me, because he still insisted on acting like we were friends and that he hadn't slept with me and then ghosted me, I calmly smiled up at him. Meanwhile, I mentally reminded myself to channel Marilyn Monroe and my own innocent, inner child.

"Actually, I'm headed back to my room but," I started and then smiled as sweetly as I could, even though I had a hell of a time ungritting my teeth. "Would you like one?"

"How can I refuse?"

I forced a laugh, while promising myself that this was the best way to deal with him. Showing anger would only make me appear like I cared too much. And I no longer cared about him at all. Yes, friendly indifference was the way to go. I held out both boxes. "Chocolate or powdered?"

"Chocolate, please."

I didn't respond but opened the box and held it out in front of him, offering him his pick. He gave me another charming smile and reached in, grabbing the donut closest to him.

"Thanks," he said as he opened his mouth and took a huge bite—huge as in only half of the thing remained.

"You're welcome." I gave him a sweet and unconcerned smile and relegated thoughts that this asshole had dumped me as soon as he'd slept with me to the back of my mind. No, thoughts like that did not and would not occupy my mind, because I was stronger than that. I was in charge of myself and I was in control of my emotions. I was cool and calculated. Calculated in as much as I'd make sure this jerkoff was taken down a peg or two.

I glanced back at my car and noticed Dani was now looking right at me. She pointed at Shit Stain 2 and made the motion of getting out of the car, as if asking me if she needed to intervene. I quickly shook my head before facing him again, hoping he hadn't noticed.

"I meant to tell you," he continued, apparently oblivious to the fact that Dani was in my car and watching us. He wiped a few crumbs off his lower lip after finishing the second half of the donut in one bite. "You've been looking really good lately."

"Thanks."

He nodded. "I kept noticing you in class, but I never said anything since we kind of... well, you know."

"No, I don't know?"

He cleared his throat. "I mean... since we sort of... ended on bad terms."

Yeah, because you were a jerk and never called me back after sleeping with me!

I maintained my breezy sensuality and smiled even more broadly. "We didn't end on bad terms," I said and waved away his comment like it was an annoying fly.

"Well, I just wanted to let you know that you're hot."

I gave him a smile in spite of myself. "Thanks.

That's really nice of you to say."

"Hey, if you aren't busy, you want to get together again? We could do a movie or dinner or just ... stay in?"

I nearly choked on his less-than-subtle insinuation about 'staying in' but managed to hold myself together. "Oh, you know, that sounds like it would be fun, but I'm actually going to be pretty busy for a while."

He frowned. "That's the excuse you gave me last time."

I sighed as I nodded. "This time it's actually true."

"I don't know how you'd be busy when school is over," he rebutted, looking confused and offended at the same time.

"Maybe for some students."

"But not you?"

I smiled broadly. "I'm actually T.A.ing for Professor Anderson over the summer."

"But you're an undergraduate." Another well pronounced frown.

"Right, but that didn't seem to faze Derek when he offered the job to me," I answered, secretly relishing the fact that my use of Derek's first name caused Beau to arch his eyebrows with unconcealed surprise.

"Derek?"

"Oh, Professor Anderson," I corrected myself.

"And my being an undergraduate didn't seem to deter him," I laughed and then shook my head. "I guess he believes I'm qualified enough."

"Or maybe he's got other motives."

You mean, like you do? I thought to myself but managed not to say anything. "Oh, I doubt it. He's a professor. I'm a student—you know how that goes."

"Just be careful, Nik." He took a step closer to me. "I would hate it if anyone ever took advantage of you."

I wanted to tell him just what I thought of him, but instead I stood up straight and tall and smiled up at him as I batted my lashes a few times. "Thanks for worrying about me, Beau, I appreciate it, but I'll be just fine." I took a quick breath and gave him a knowing smile. "I can handle Derek." He arched a brow and took a step closer to me. I immediately glanced at my cell phone. "I really have to get going now." I took a step towards the car. "I'm really glad I ran into you though. It was really nice to see you."

"I'm going to let you go for now," he answered, talking a little louder because I'd already started making my way toward my car. "But I'm going to call you for dinner this week."

"Okay."

There's no way I'll ever go out with you again, I swore to myself as I unlocked the car door, and handing the donut boxes to Dani, said underneath my breath, "some guys just won't get the hint."

"I'm really happy I saw you, Nikki," Shit Stain 2 continued as he started toward the store but continued looking back at me. He glanced at Dani momentarily and gave her a little, surprised wave, like he'd only just noticed she was there.

I seated myself behind the wheel and waved to him as I started the engine. He waved back, then disappeared inside the store.

"You okay?" Dani asked as she faced me with concern.

"Yeah, I'm fine." I gave her a big smile. "I'm actually more than fine."

I'd handled the whole situation perfectly. I hadn't come off as bitter or angry and, instead, I'd rekindled Beau's interest by playing attentive yet occupied. Keep up the game and he'd be eating out of my hand soon enough—well, if I wanted him to. And I didn't. But maybe I'd play with him just because I could. Jane would be proud.

"What were you talking about?" Dani asked as I backed out of the parking spot and headed toward the main street that led back towards the school.

"Um, he asked me out again."

"What?" Dani's mouth dropped open. "What an asshole!"

"Yep."

"So... what did you say?"

"Just that I was busy."

"And what did he say?"

"That he'd call me next week and some crap about me looking really hot lately."

"And what did you say?"

I shrugged as I pulled up to a red light and turned to face her. "I said thanks."

"What?" she asked with a frown. "Don't tell me you're going to consider dating him again…"

"No, no, no," I interrupted, shaking my head. "I'm playing the game, Dani, that's all this is. I'm going to turn the tables on him, like Jane would want me to do."

"Ohhhh," Dani nodded as a big smile beamed across her face. "You smart, conniving bitch."

We both laughed as I pulled into the drive-thru at McDonald's. We rarely ate hamburgers, but I suddenly had a craving.

"Um, what are we doing at McDonald's?" Dani asked.

"I've got this incredible craving for French fries and a strawberry shake."

"Hmm, that does sound good, but make mine a chocolate shake." She took a breath. "I think you deserve fries, a shake and plenty of donuts after that spectacular performance with Shit Stain, the second."

I laughed. "I have to agree."

After we ordered and drove through to pick up

and pay, I pulled out onto the street and headed for the park which was right next to campus. It was well past midnight when we sat down at one of the picnic tables near the swings and dug into our well-deserved food.

"This is so going to give me a zit," Dani said. "But, oh, my God, it's been so long since we did this."

"I know." But I couldn't say my attention was on the conversation. Instead, I couldn't stop replaying the conversation I'd just had with Beau. Suddenly, I wasn't sure if I really was doing the right thing. I mean, who was to say that everything in the notebook was really something worth following? Yes, it seemed to make sense, but who was Jane really? How did we really know if everything she'd written was even true? What if it was just some big psychology experiment—to see what would happen if someone randomly found the notebook? I swallowed hard at that thought.

"Dani?" I asked as I sucked down a few gulps of my shake.

"Yeah?"

"Do you think we're doing the right thing?"

"What do you mean?"

I shrugged. "I don't know. It just occurred to me that maybe the notebook is just bullshit."

"What?" Dani sounded like I'd just told her the earth wasn't round.

"I mean, I feel like that notebook has definitely helped me to regain control of my life, but what if the opposite is actually true? What if we're way too concerned with controlling men now and, in Beau's case, revenge? What if the whole thing was just some experiment put on by the psychology department and it was never meant to be taken seriously?"

"Um, I have no idea what conspiracy theories you've been reading about lately, but I'm pretty sure the psychology department has nothing to do with Jane's notebook."

I swallowed hard. "My point is: what if the notebook is wrong? What if Jane doesn't know what she's talking about and what if we're just making a big mistake?"

Dani was quiet for a few seconds as she considered it. Then she shook her head. "I don't look at it that way at all. And I don't think you should either."

"I'm just wondering if we're playing with fire by following what the handbook says. I mean—it's not proven. Jane Doe isn't even a real name." I piled a few fries into my mouth.

"I think you're having a moment of guilt after your interaction with Beau," Dani answered with a quick nod. "But what I would point out is that he used you for sex and then dumped you on your ass."

"Yes, I guess that's true. But does that make what I'm planning on doing to him right?"

"What are you planning on doing to him?"

I shrugged—what was I planning on doing to him? "I don't know. I guess I just want to wrap him around my finger so I can treat him the way he treated me. Well, minus the sex part."

"Okay," Dani dove into a powdered donut and then licked the white sugar off her lips. "And are you forcing him in some way to fall for you?"

"I don't even know if he *will* fall for me."

"Let's just say, for the sake of argument, that you seduce him and he totally falls for everything you do, hook, line and sinker."

"Okay."

"The point is: he's doing so by the freedom of his own will, right?" I nodded and she continued. "So, as far as I can tell, you aren't forcing him to act or to think a certain way. If he's gullible enough to fall for you and you play him, then that's his own problem. Just like it was your own problem for sleeping with him and getting dumped."

"You have a blunt way of putting things." But she was right.

"Mean what you say and say what you mean." She shrugged. "And regarding the femme fatale, Jane stuff, you said yourself that it made you feel freer and more in control of your life, right?" I nodded again. "So, that can't be all bad, can it?"

I sighed as I thought about it. She was right in that I did feel like I was more in control of my life. I also felt more confident. "I guess you're right. It can't be all bad. I mean, we're becoming more self-confident and we aren't letting guys treat us the way they used to. I also feel like I'm more in control of my emotions too, so maybe I'm looking at this wrong."

"I think so." She dipped back into her basket of fries. "You are woman, hear you roar, remember?"

I laughed as I remembered my meeting with Derek earlier. "So, I took Derek up on the position of his assistant."

She smiled. "That will definitely make seducing him easier."

I nodded as I remembered his smile when we were teasing each other and how easy our interaction had been. There was definitely something there between us—some sort of energy sizzling just under the surface. I could feel it and I was pretty sure he could feel it too. "It's weird but I'm sort of looking forward to seducing him."

"Why is that weird?" She frowned at me. "You must have finally realized how hot he is?"

I cocked my head to the side as I considered it. "I've always known he was a good looking guy so I'm not sure it's that."

"Then you do think he's good looking because

for a while there, you wouldn't even admit that."

I smiled at her. "I can admit he's... *pretty* good looking."

"Nikki, he's hot."

"Okay, he's hot." I shook my head as I laughed at her expression. "But that's not why I think it might be fun to use him as my target, like Jane calls him." I shook my head again as I tried to pinpoint the exact reason. "There's just something else about him that makes me laugh. It's almost like he's got this boyish charm that's exasperating at the same time that it's kind of ... cute."

"Uh oh."

"What do you mean—uh oh?"

"Don't go falling for your target." She gave me a serious expression, all humor missing from her tone. "Remember that, Nikki—that's rule number one."

"Oh, my God, I'm not going to fall for him." I was irritated that she'd even think that was a possibility. Not only was Derek a professor, but he was also way too old for me—maybe that's why he was safe as a target—because there was no way anything would ever happen between us. He might as well have been on another planet.

"Okay, just wanted to make sure," Dani said as she studied me with narrowed eyes. "Remember why you're doing this."

"Right." Then I looked at her. "Remind me

why I'm doing this?"

She sighed and pretended to be exasperated. "To prove to yourself and to me that it really works. And if you get a boyfriend out of it, all the better I guess."

"A boyfriend? Derek isn't going to be my boyfriend. Jesus."

"Keep telling yourself that," she answered as she sucked the last of her chocolate shake through the straw and I frowned at her. "No, I mean it—keep telling yourself that. Because the moment you get attached and give up the game, that's the moment you lose."

THREE
The Femme Fatale Handbook
Chapter Eight: Keep Him Guessing

What's the number one killer to a successful seduction and to relationships in general?
Boredom.
Once he loses interest in you or guesses your game, you're no longer playing it. So, how do we make sure that doesn't happen? It's easy—you have to keep him on his toes. Don't ever let him figure you out.

Most people wear their emotions on their sleeves which makes them sooo easy to figure out. Be the opposite. Be a contradiction. Be someone unpredictable—someone not easily figured out.

Test—if someone is able to describe you in a word or two, that means it's time to change it up. If people think of you as overly sensitive, get a tougher exterior. If you're usually the joking, takes-nothing-too-seriously person, develop a pensive and thoughtful side. If you're usually timid and naive about everything, learn how to find your own inner cunning. Whatever you are, learn to enable the opposite.

And remember, it's not enough to capture his interest with a sexy outfit, a provocative glance or a seductive smile. That's just the beginning—just tricks of the trade to get him to make the first move. The key is to capture him, to ensnare him with your magical spell and keep him enthralled—keep him stuck in your web, and the only way you can do that is through your personality.

Make him think there's more to you than what he sees on the surface. Men love to figure things out. They're driven to conquer, and what better way to placate that instinct than to supply them with a riddle they think they can figure out but never actually do?

The key to keeping him on his toes and forever guessing is not something you need to work on over time. It needs to happen as soon as you both open your mouths and initiate conversation. What does that mean? It means sending mixed signals from the start, that way he doesn't jump to conclusions about you, conclusions which are usually very hard to break.

Within those first few minutes of meeting you, maybe he starts to formulate the opinion that you're confident, funny and smart, but then you pique his interest by very subtly hinting at a shy or devilish side to your personality. Or maybe you seem studious at the start? Then hint at something daring and naughty that lurks just underneath the surface.

And don't be afraid to be a little bad. Not all your characteristics need to be good ones. When was the last time you fell in love with a hero in a romance novel who was entirely good? Never, right? Instead, you fell for the rogue with the questionable background who wants to be better than he is, but somehow he just can't seem to ignore his baser, lustful and animalistic nature.

The same thing goes for men in real life. They won't be drawn in by the innocent prairie girl with the braids who's only thinking about marriage. They will, however, be drawn in by the innocent girl with the devilish glint in her eyes who seems shy but then drops a few hints that she's anything but.

###
NIKKI

"So, I've discovered one drawback to all of this seduction stuff," I said as I took a sip of my margarita and chomped on a tortilla chip loaded with guacamole.

Dani and I were having dinner at a local Mexican restaurant, Guadalupe's. In about three hours, all the tables in the bar would be cleared in favor of a dance floor.

"Oh?" Dani asked. "What's that?"

"I'm horny!" I responded with a little laugh. "I mean, teasing is fine and good, but I'm pretty sure I'm going to get sick of tending to my own sexual needs. It's like all this stuff we've been doing is drumming up this need inside me that I didn't even realize I had."

Dani shrugged as she appeared to think about it. "Well, that brings up a good question."

"It does?"

"I mean... do you think it goes against the rules for us to have a lover?"

"Um," I started and frowned at her.

She held up a hand. "Just hear me out for a second—what if we have a lover who's just used for that? Like he's just used for the express purpose of satisfying our sexual needs and nothing else?"

I took a swallow of my margarita and was quiet as I considered her question. "I guess it wouldn't be against the rules." Or would it? I had to think about it for another couple of second. "I guess... as long as we didn't want anything serious with him."

"Hmm... because I kind of wanted to nail that guy last night." She was talking about some guy we'd met while we were working out at the school gym.

"They're the ones who are supposed to do the nailing," I laughed. "You don't have the hammer or the nail."

She gave me a look. "I'm serious, dude—I'm basically like cock-blocking myself."

"Vag-blocking?"

She made another face. "That sounds like an STD or something you can catch."

I laughed but then nodded. "I know what you're getting at though. It's like you want some sort of relief—like there's all this buildup but no release."

She nodded. "Exactly! I mean, we have all these cute guys we're talking to and we can't do anything with them. It's like being a kid in a toy store and you aren't allowed to play with any of the toys."

"True, but I guess we could always go back to the way we used to be where we were getting action but then getting dumped." I shrugged. "We're the ones who decided to do this, right? It's not like anyone forced us."

"Ugh," Dani grumbled. "I hate it when you talk all devil's advocate on me." I munched another chip and took the last remaining blob of guacamole. "Thanks for hogging all the guac, by the way."

"It's not my fault you were talking too much and missed out," I laughed. "Besides, shouldn't you be the one who should be telling me all the reasons why we should be doing this, Ms. Psychology Degree?"

I was referring to the fact that Dani was in the process of getting her degree in psychology. "Swallow that mouthful so I don't have to continue to be grossed out and maybe I'll tell you what I think."

I smiled as I downed the offending bite with a gulp of margarita and then faced her expectantly. "I love it when you put your soon-to-be psychology degree to practice."

"So do I, because it reminds me that all this money I'm spending on my education is actually worth a damn. Not that figuring out your sexual frustration is of any economical advantage to me …"

"So what? Get to the good stuff."

She gave me a look. "I think you're channeling

your inner man."

"Um, what?" But we were interrupted when the waiter stopped in front of our table and unloaded a plate of enchiladas in front of me and a taco salad in front of Dani. We thanked him, and once he walked away, she continued.

"Think about it—we aren't playing traditional roles anymore."

"We aren't?"

She shook her head. "We aren't playing our usual roles of trying to get a guy into a relationship. Instead, we've adopted the male role of playing hard to get."

"Okay, I'm following you so far, I think."

"So, in suddenly being in the advantageous position of having all the power and control, and the subsequent boost to your self-confidence, I think you've channeled some of the male sex drive?"

"Okay."

"You're now in the position of the dominant, and that's probably what's making you so horny." She shrugged. "Well, me too, for that matter."

"Wow." I leaned back into my seat, my eyebrows reaching for the ceiling. "Freud would be proud."

"I'm serious, Nik," she said with a laugh as she dug into her salad. "I think our sense of confidence is making us want to... mate."

"Mate? Really? Could you think of any other word for it that doesn't sound so Animal Kingdom?"

She laughed. "Animal Kingdom aside, it's a good argument, don't you think?"

I nodded. "Yeah, I buy it. But regardless of whether I'm channeling my inner man, it doesn't change the fact that I want a man in my inner channel."

Dani nearly choked on her lettuce.

"Are you okay over here, or do I need to pull out my Heimlich skills?" A deep, rich voice sounded from behind me. I turned around to see Derek standing there with one of his friends, Luke, I thought his name was.

I downed my bite and then smiled while I hoped there wasn't anything in my teeth.

"Hi, Derek," I said as Dani greeted them at the same time.

I wasn't sure why but I was totally flushed all over—it was like as soon as I'd seen Derek, my body temperature increased by like a hundred degrees. Maybe it was because he wasn't dressed in his professor best, and instead was wearing dark blue jeans and a white t-shirt and I could see the lines of his pecs and the outline of his nipples? I swallowed hard and tried to keep my eyes on his.

"You remember Luke?" Derek asked as he faced his friend.

"Of course," Dani answered. "How could we forget Luke?" Then she gave him an encouraging smile which just wreaked of Mae West. Right—our parts. Currently, I wasn't playing mine at all. I took a deep breath and remembered myself.

"The question is, do you remember Dani?" I managed as she threw me a faux cross look.

"How could anyone forget me?" she asked, arching her brows haughtily.

"I was about to ask the same," Luke agreed with a laugh as he took a step closer to her. Hmm, maybe this one would prove to be a good candidate for Dani's seduction…

"Do you mind if we sit?" Derek asked me. "Otherwise, the wait list is twenty minutes."

"Sucks to be you," I laughed as I shook my head and took a purposeful bite of my enchilada. "Mmm, this is sooo good, and it's so much better enjoying it with all this room on either side of me." I actually stretched my arms out to further annoy him.

"Scoot over, asshole," Derek said as he sat down next to me and forcefully shoved his hip against mine, pushing me into the corner of the booth.

Dani tapped the open booth next to her and smiled up at Luke. "Are you mooches hungry too?"

"Maybe a little," Derek answered while he reached over, grabbed my fork from my fingers and speared a bite of enchilada as I looked up at him in surprise.

"Hey!" I started and smacked him playfully.

"So, Nik here tells me she's going to be your assistant?" Dani asked as she faced Derek.

"That's the plan." Then he looked at me. "You weren't lying—this thing is good."

I just frowned at him and motioned for him to give me my fork back but all he did was took another bite of my dinner. I was about call him on it but I focused on someone standing behind Luke, and the words caught in my throat as my stomach dropped down to my toes.

###
DEREK

Dani turned around, following Nikki's gaze, and she swallowed hard.

I looked up and noticed a man standing there.

He wasn't alone.

He was standing at the front of the restaurant, talking to the hostess, and there was a leggy redhead next to him. She was wearing so much makeup, she looked like a clown.

I turned back to face Nikki and noticed all the color had drained out of her face. She looked like she'd just seen a ghost.

"What's wrong?" I asked in a soft voice as I

faced Dani in confusion, hoping I could get an answer from her, because Nikki looked comatose.

Dani didn't say anything right away, almost as if she wasn't sure if Nikki wanted her to. I raised my eyebrows at her once it was obvious that neither one of them was going to respond.

"Um," Dani started.

"Really?" Nikki said underneath her breath, her gaze still focused on the man standing in the entryway. She reached for her margarita and downed a few gulps as seconds later, I felt someone walk past me and then the guy was standing at our table, the redhead just beside him. They were holding hands.

"Nik," he said in greeting and then glanced at Dani. "Dani, good to see you both."

"Wish I could say the same," Dani answered with a cheery smile before forcefully taking a bite of her salad, apparently so she wouldn't have to say anything else.

"Hi, Brandon," Nikki said, trying her best to appear cool and calm. But there was something about the way she said the words that said she was anything but.

"We were standing in line, waiting for a table, and I noticed you over here so thought I'd come over and say hi," the guy explained as his attention fell to me. He reached out and offered his hand. "I'm Brandon, nice to meet you."

I took it although I eyed him narrowly, not liking the fact that he was getting such a reaction from Nikki. Obviously, they knew each other, but there was also definitely something much bigger going on between the two of them. "Derek," I answered.

"And I'm Luke," Luke said as he extended his hand.

"I'm Gina," the redheaded clown said with a wide smile that showed too much gum. She waved at all of us and Nikki smiled back, although I could see her mouth twitching which had to mean she was anything but comfortable.

"Hey, aren't you a professor?" Brandon asked as he faced me.

"Yes," I answered and then met Brandon's eyes, not wanting to appear in any way like I felt guilty to be hanging out with Nikki. Not that I should have, but it was a bit of an awkward situation, all the same.

"Yeah, I think I had you for a class a couple semesters ago," Brandon continued.

"Cool," I said, my body language and disinterest in general begging the question as to why Brandon was still standing here when it was pretty clear he wasn't welcome.

Brandon's gaze traveled to Nikki and then back to me and his slight frown hinted that he wasn't sure if we were a couple or not. Then he smiled. "Well, have a good night. Was nice to see you, Nik."

"You too," she answered with a cheery smile that I was more than sure she didn't really feel.

"Bye!" Gina chirped as they walked away.

"He was the last person I expected to see here," Dani started as she faced Nikki and tried to ascertain whether or not she was okay. "Wasn't he supposed to be in Phoenix or something?"

"Yeah," Nikki answered as she faced me. She was pale. "Would you mind getting up, Derek? I need to run to the restroom."

I didn't respond other than to stand up as she smiled at me and, grabbing her purse, she started for the bathroom. I considered following her, but then I thought better of it because I wasn't sure if she trusted me enough to open up about what had just happened or who this Brandon guy was to her. Instead, I faced Dani with an expression that begged an explanation.

She sighed. "So that was Nikki's ex-boyfriend..."

"Ah, okay," Luke said. "I was wondering why it seemed like she swallowed her tongue as soon as he walked over here."

"How long ago did they break up?" I asked, a sinking feeling developing in the pit of my stomach. Clearly, he still meant something to her, owing to her reaction. And I was more than sure it hadn't helped that he was with another woman.

Dani shrugged. "Maybe a few months ago? As you can probably guess, it wasn't an easy breakup for her. They were together since her freshman year."

I nodded. "He seemed like a douche."

"He is a douche," she said with a laugh.

"So, what's the story then?" I asked after I noticed Dani texting a few times on her phone. No doubt, she was checking on Nikki.

"She said she's fine," Dani said with an encouraging smile as she put her phone down again. "And she'll be back in a second."

"Okay, that's good," I answered.

When Nikki walked back down the hallway, the color was back in her cheeks and her eye makeup looked intact, so I didn't think she'd been in there crying, thank God. She smiled at me, ostensibly to affirm that she really was okay. I stood up and smiled down at her as she nodded at me and then took her seat.

"So, what were we talking about?" she asked as she faced the three of us expectantly.

###

It was maybe another hour that we sat there.

Luke ordered a taco plate and I finished Nikki's enchiladas because it seemed like seeing

Brandon had taken her appetite away. But it hadn't taken her appetite for alcohol away, and by the end of the hour, she'd downed another huge margarita. When the bill came, I paid it (even though everyone tried to argue) and then helped Nikki to her feet as she swayed.

"How'd you guys get here?" I asked Dani.

"We walked."

"Okay, I'll give you a ride back," I said as Dani thanked me and we started toward the front of the restaurant, Nikki and I leading the way. As soon as we turned the corner, I noticed Brandon and Gina were sitting in a booth just beside the door. I felt myself cringe at the prospect that Brandon would realize that Nikki was totally and completely drunk. She definitely wasn't walking straight.

So as we approached their table, I put my arm around Nikki and pulled her into me and she wrapped her arms around my waist. Brandon saw the whole thing, and his frown spoke volumes. Yep, he was definitely a douche.

FOUR
NIKKI

I was aware that I was drunk.

But I couldn't say I really cared because I was still trying to triage the damage that had happened to me when I'd seen Brandon. And it wasn't just seeing Brandon, but seeing him with some chick—well, I had to admit it had hurt. The truth was, I was still reeling on the inside—but more from the shock of it than the pain of it.

Although there was a part of me that was disappointed at how I'd reacted, how my stomach had dropped to my toes and I'd instantly felt sick, there was another part of me that couldn't stop thinking about the way Derek had wrapped his arm around me so protectively. It was like he'd totally understood what I was going through and he'd responded by acting the part of my boyfriend—right in front of Brandon. Not only that, but Brandon had definitely noticed it. I'd seen how his eyes watched us while we walked to the front door, and I'd felt his eyes on us once my back was facing him.

In some strange and small way, Derek had saved me. I know that sounded totally ridiculous, but it was true. At least, it was true in my own eyes.

In just putting his arm around my shoulders and pulling me close to him, he'd totally evened the playing field between Brandon and me—like Brandon had moved on, but so had I. And I was grateful to Derek, beyond grateful, really.

As Derek pulled up to the ZTS house, I heard Dani unbuckling her seat belt from where she was sitting next to Luke and I turned to face her. "Would you guys mind if I chatted with Derek for a second?"

Dani looked a little surprised but then nodded.

"Sure, I'll walk Dani to her room," Luke said as he unbuckled his belt and they both stepped out of Derek's Bronco.

I smiled at my roommate and best friend.

"Thanks, I'll be up in a sec."

"Okay," she answered as her gaze shifted to Derek.

"I'll make sure she gets up to her room safe and sound," he answered her unasked question as she nodded. Then she closed the door behind her, and Luke escorted her up the walkway to the stairs and into the sorority house. I took a deep breath as my head began to ache with the copious amounts of alcohol I'd consumed.

"Thanks for doing what you did tonight," I said as I turned to Derek.

It was beyond weird, but as I looked at him, I almost felt like I was looking at him for the first time—like I was just now taking in the fact that his hair was too long and there was shadow covering his jaw and chin. I took in those beautiful, large eyes and the square lines of his chin, his aquiline nose and I felt something different towards him. Usually, it was a mix of irritation and a certain level of attraction that I felt towards him. Now, though, it was admiration mixed with a hell of a lot of attraction...

"What did I do tonight?" he asked with a smile as he cranked on the heat and then held his hand in front of the vent to make sure it was working.

"You know, the part where you put your arm around me in front of Brandon," I said, suddenly feeling self-conscious and stupid as I wondered if I was making way more out of something that was simply a quick act to help out a friend who was obviously in an uncomfortable spot. "I just... well, I wanted to tell you that I appreciate it."

"Just doing my part to make sure you weren't going to trip and fall on your ass." He shrugged with a light chuckle.

I nodded as I replayed the events of the night in my head, especially the part when I'd first seen Brandon and ... Gina. Yes, I was shocked and yes it had hurt, but somehow, and I wasn't sure how, it hadn't hurt as much as I would have thought it would. I mean, the pain was still there, sure, but it wasn't fully encompassing. It was really more the shock that had done a number on me.

"You want me to walk you up now?" Derek asked as he faced me expectantly.

"No, not yet." I ran my fingers across the fabric of the seat as I remembered the tall brunette Derek had been with at the library the night he'd given me a ride back to the ZTS house. I also remembered how she'd insisted I sit in the backseat. It had been obvious that she'd had the hots for him. I just wasn't sure then and wasn't sure now how *he* felt about *her*.

"That dark-haired girl I met," I started as I turned toward him. "I think her name was Rebecca?"

"Yeah, what about her?" He frowned, like she

was the last person he wanted to talk about.

"Was or is she your girlfriend?"

Derek immediately laughed and shook his head. "No, it's nothing like that."

"So why did she act so... territorial with you?"

Derek's gaze settled on the steering wheel as he sighed before glancing back at me. When his eyes met mine, I was again overcome by how handsome he was. I was almost floored by it. How hadn't I noticed it to this extent before? I'd somehow convinced myself that I wasn't interested in him. Maybe because I was intimidated by him? He definitely had a bold confidence that was intimidating.

Yeah, and super sexy.

As I looked at him, I felt the bubbling of something inside me, deep down. Something that felt like a stinging, yearning need deep inside me. And then I had the brief vision of Derek's lips on mine, his fingers on my breasts...

"Rebecca has never been shy about her feelings for me," he said, his voice pulling me out of my thoughts.

"Oh."

He sighed again, like he didn't like thinking about it or her.

"And what about you?" I asked.

He shrugged. "Some of the rumors you've heard about me are true."

"Does that mean you slept with her?" I was surprised by my own boldness in asking the question because it was clearly none of my business.

"Maybe," he answered as he looked over at me and raised a brow. "Not that that's any business of yours, drunk ass." He chuckled and then poked my shoulder with his index finger playfully, but his eyes stayed fastened on mine a little too long, *a lot* too long actually. In fact, we were staring at each other so obviously, it probably looked like we were in the middle of a staring contest.

"I'm not that drunk," I insisted, but my voice was breathy.

"You're so drunk, you can't even walk straight." Derek shook his head and chuckled. "And speaking of, I should probably get you back to your room so Dani doesn't start to worry about what we're doing down here."

"What are we doing down here?" I asked immediately, suddenly wanting and needing more from him. Actually, the need was so thick inside me, I felt like I was choking on it.

But he shook his head. "Nothing."

I don't know what came over me then—maybe it was the alcohol that was fueling whatever this was that I was feeling, but I absolutely refused to acknowledge his response. Instead, I unbuckled my seat belt, feeling a flush of bravado rushing through me. Apparently thinking I was ready to go, Derek unbuckled his belt too and reached for the handle on the door.

"Maybe we *should* be doing something," I said as I leaned over and put my hand on his thigh. I started to lean into him as our eyes met and his were filled with a fire I'd only seen that day in the classroom when we'd argued and I'd walked away but he'd immediately pulled me back to him.

"What do you think we should be doing?" His voice was gruff and I felt his hands encircle my waist as I leaned further into him and lifted my face to his. Before I could even think another thought, his mouth was on mine and mine was on his. I opened my lips to him and his tongue was suddenly in my mouth. He tasted and felt so good, I heard myself moan and, in response, he tightened his hold around my waist. Never breaking my lips from his, I freed myself from my belt and swung my leg over the middle console so I could climb into his lap.

I was beyond wet at this point, and I could feel that stinging sensation deep in my core. Not only that, but my nipples were hard as rocks. Every part of my body was screaming at me, telling me I wanted and needed Derek inside me. Truly, that was the only thought in my head.

Until he pulled his face away and brought both of his hands to my arms, pushing me back.

"We... we can't do this, Nikki." As he faced me, his eyebrows met in the center of his forehead and he frowned. But he was also breathing so hard, he appeared to almost be panting and that fire was still there in his eyes. "I'm … I'm sorry I kissed you."

"Don't be sorry." I meant the words, wanting nothing more than to feel his lips on mine again. I could feel his cock underneath me and it was hard, straining against his jeans. He wanted me; no matter what he was saying. His body was saying something entirely different.

I started to reach for him again but he held me back. "No, Nikki, this isn't how I want things between us." Now when I looked at him, that burning desire I'd seen in his eyes was replaced with something else—stern determination. I felt my heart drop.

"Oh." A rush of humiliation flooded me and I suddenly couldn't look at him.

"Fuck," he muttered as he tilted my chin up, forcing me to look him in the eyes. "That's not how I meant it." He breathed in hard and shook his head as he ran a hand through his hair. When he looked at me again, I could see the fight in his eyes. "I want you—you must know I want you."

"You're saying you don't."

He shook his head. "The truth is that I want nothing more than to tear your clothes off and take you right here, but that's not how things can or should be between us. You know that as well as I do."

I nodded but couldn't say anything because of the lump in my throat. I was a total idiot. I'd just forced myself on him and he didn't want me. First Brandon, then Beau, and now Derek. What the fuck was wrong with me? Everything I'd learned in the handbook, all the training I'd studied—I'd just screwed it all up.

Derek didn't say anything more, but opened his door and jumped down to the ground. I caught him adjusting himself, and when I glanced at his pants, I could see his dick still straining against them. The guy was as hard as hard could be, and what was more, it looked like his cock was enormous. And yet he wasn't willing to give it to me. He didn't want me. And, for the life of me, I couldn't understand why. I mean—it went against everything I'd ever heard about guys—they were all supposed to just want sex. And Derek had basically admitted to his bad-boy reputation and yet... yet, he didn't want me.

But he just said he wanted you, I argued with myself, all the while just believing he was saving face in saying what he had. The truth was—if he wanted me, he would have taken me. Especially after I'd basically just served myself up to him on a platter.

I opened my door as I wondered how in the hell I was going to face him after this. I was completely and totally mortified at the thought of just having to look into his face and see an expression of pity there. This would have to go down as the most embarrassing night of my life.

He walked around the Bronco and held my door open for me, reaching out and taking my hand as he assisted me down to the cold asphalt below. Then he took my elbow when I tripped over my own feet, and I was further humiliated because he was right—I was so drunk, I couldn't even stand up, let alone walk.

"I'm so embarrassed," I said finally, once the frog in my throat hopped back down into my stomach.

"Don't be." He patted me on the back like I was a kid. "Just get a good night's sleep and remember that tomorrow is a new day."

Tomorrow.

I couldn't even stomach the idea of how I'd feel in the morning, when I didn't have the delirium of inebriation to soften my mortification.

I didn't say anything, but I allowed Derek to help me up the stairs and through the double entry doors of the sorority house. Luckily, no one was milling around the living room or the kitchen which was just off the entryway. The last thing I wanted right now was an audience.

As soon as we reached the bottom of the stairs, Dani appeared with Luke in the hallway above us. She immediately came down and took my other arm as Derek released me. Luke was right behind her.

"Thanks for your help," she said to Derek as she smiled with obvious gratitude. "I can take her the rest of the way."

"No problem," Derek answered. "Hope you feel better, Nikki."

"Thanks," I grumbled as I leaned into Dani and took a deep breath, trying to force my tears back. The last thing I wanted to do was make this embarrassment even worse by crying in front of him.

I heard the sound of Derek's and Luke's footsteps on the hardwood floors and then the sound of the door closing behind them. By that time, we'd reached our room, and Dani opened the door as I fell onto my bed and the sobs came. She closed the door behind her and then she was by my side, her hand on my back.

"It's okay, Nik, it's going to be okay."

"No, it isn't!" I wailed as I reprimanded myself for being so stupid. I'd completely disregarded everything Jane had said; I'd disregarded everything I'd learned in *The Femme Fatale Handbook,* and this was my punishment. This was what I got when I threw myself at a man who didn't want me.

"You're over him, you know you are," Dani started as I wondered what the hell she was talking about. "Don't let this set you back. You were just fine before you saw him."

"I'm not talking about Brandon!" I railed back at her, suddenly angry that we weren't on the same page. "I don't care about Brandon," I continued as I wiped my eyes with my sleeve and hiccupped.

"Then what?" She shook her head and faced me in total confusion.

I didn't even want to say it, the words were so despicable. "I just came onto Derek and he pushed me away!" She cringed slightly, and that was when it hit me that I'd totally fucked up. I collapsed against my bed in a new fit of tears as I bemoaned my own horrible luck.

"That's not that... terrible, Nik," Dani said as she resumed rubbing my back.

"Bullshit, Dani, it's terrible and you know it!"

"No, it's not."

I looked up at her. "And how in the hell do you figure that?"

She shrugged. "There's no way he was going to do anything with you in his car with Luke and me in here and you as drunk as you are! Actually, he did the right thing."

I stopped crying and started listening to her because maybe she had a point. "He did?"

"Yes! What he did—it was the nice guy thing to do."

"So you don't think I totally messed up?"

"No," she answered as she shook her head and smiled at me. "But, just for the sake of curiosity, what did he say or do after he pushed you away?"

"Um," I tried to remember, which wasn't easy because everything was sort of clouded with the jelly of inebriation. "He said he did want me but that we couldn't do this. I told him I was totally embarrassed and he told me not to be. He told me to get some sleep and that tomorrow was a new day." I took a breath. "Then he patted me on the back like I was his dog or something."

Dani laughed. "I would believe him, Nikki. Tomorrow, everything is going to be fine."

"It doesn't feel like it's going to be fine," I grumbled. "And what if he tells Luke that I threw myself at him?"

"He won't. I don't think Derek would do that to you. He respects you way too much."

"Respects me?"

"Yeah, why else would he have come to your rescue by putting his arm around you when we walked past Brandon?"

"He said he did it because he was afraid I was going to trip."

"Total and complete bullshit." Dani shook her head. "He said that because he's proud and he didn't want to admit that he was saving you."

"You think?"

She nodded. "What he did wasn't about helping you walk straight, dummy. He was pretending to be your boyfriend, Nik," she continued, frowning at me like I should have been smart enough to figure this out on my own. "I watched him when he did it, and he looked right at Brandon in, like, a challenging way." She took a breath. "I don't believe for a second that he was just doing it so you wouldn't nosedive in front of everyone."

"Well, either way, he probably hates me now." I sniffled. I was sure I'd leaked snot all over my bed, but at this point, I couldn't say I even cared.

"He doesn't hate you. There's no way that man could ever hate you. I saw the way he looks at you and the way he teases you. He's smitten."

"He's not smitten," I argued as I shook my head. "He said we couldn't do anything together."

"Probably because he's a professor and you're his T.A. That doesn't mean he doesn't want to though."

"Whatever it means doesn't matter." I shook my head as I threw my hands into the air. "Now I'm going to have to start all over again."

"With what?"

"Finding a new target." I wiped my nose across my sleeve and Dani frowned at me like I was pretty disgusting. Then she stood up and reached for the box of tissues she kept beside her bed.

"Use these 'cause you're grossing me out," she said as she shoved them at me.

I took one and dutifully blew my nose. Then I threw the wet clump of tissue into the trash can as I faced her. "I totally blew everything I'd been working towards."

"What did you blow?"

"My training!" I railed at her, irritated that she still wasn't following me. "Jane said we should never get too drunk that we don't make good decisions, and look what I did! In one evening, I just undid everything I've worked so hard for!"

Dani shook her head. "You're being way too dramatic. All hope isn't lost." Then she reached down and started unbuckling my strappy shoes. "What you need to do is get a good night's sleep, and tomorrow we will come up with a course of action, a plan."

I yawned in spite of myself and assisted her in taking my clothes off. She walked to our dresser and, reaching into the bottom drawer, pulled out my pink Victoria's Secret jammies, handing them to me. I put them on and then climbed under my covers, suddenly feeling exhausted.

"Thanks for being such a good BFF," I said as my head hit the pillow.

"You're welcome." She got undressed and then

put her nightgown on. Then she padded over to her bed and climbed under the covers. "I'm sure I'll be playing this role soon enough. Although let's hope I don't try to attack a guy in his car in front of ZTS while my best friend is waiting for my sorry, drunk ass."

I had to laugh, because it was the only thing left to do.

FIVE
The Femme Fatale Handbook
Chapter Nine: Be Popular!

When I titled this chapter, I didn't mean that you need to get out there and make a ton of new friends in order to win popularity contests.

Well, sort of.

What I mean is this: men, and people in general, think something is worth more when other people also want it. Translated, that means a man wants to know you're wanted by more than just him. He wants to know that you're a prize he had to wrestle away from other men.

Need an example? Think about an auction. Have you ever seen people at an auction get into a frenzy about winning something when multiple people start betting on it? Whatever it was that they were betting on in the first place suddenly no longer matters, the importance becomes the action of winning against other bidders.

Think about the restaurant business. Imagine a new restaurant opens up nearby, but you notice it's always empty, what would you imagine the food was like? Probably not good, right? In general, restaurants that are brimming with patrons only attract more patrons. Why? Because people figure that if other people like the food there, it must be good. Well, the same rule applies to people. If other men want to spend time with you, there must be a reason why. If you're in high demand, a man will notice it and he'll want you more.

Seduction follows similar rules. A man wants to feel like he won you—that you are a prize highly valued by other men. He wants the ego boost of knowing you have many options, many guys to choose from and yet you choose to spend your valuable time with him. It's basically self-validation—proof that he must be pretty darn special in order to have won your affections, someone who has many other choices. But, the key to remember here, is that he will never win your affections entirely. Not if you're a true femme fatale. He might win your attention for a day or so, but there will always be other men waiting in the wings. And he knows this, which is why he constantly competes for your attention.

So how do you become popular when the only company you have are the crickets chirping in your room? Simple, reach out to male friends in your circle, and if you don't have any, make some. If you've been neglecting your social life, now is the time to focus on it wholeheartedly. Any and all men are viable subjects as long as they aren't related to you. Think friends, ex-boyfriends, would-be boyfriends, the guy you met at the supermarket last week, the cute guy who always helps you at the post office, get creative! It's time to build your reputation as a woman men want to be around. It's time to get the object of your interest to compete for your attention!

Don't put all your eggs in one basket! Why is this important? For the following reasons:

1. It prevents you from stressing over one particular guy. The more men you have at your disposal, the less attached you'll get to just one.

2. The more the merrier! Why settle for just one guy, when you can play with more? You'll feel better about yourself as well. Think about it—having lots of guys reaching out to you? Talk about a confidence boost!

3. You'll look better to him. If you have multiple men vying for your attention, he's going to realize he has to up his game in order to win you. You become someone more highly valued.

4. It reminds you that you have options so you can dump any guy who isn't living up to your expectations. If you have choices, you don't have to stick with one guy if he isn't working out.

5. It levels the playing field... if he's desirable to you, he's probably desirable to other women, which means he has options. So, shouldn't you have options as well? The answer is yes!

###
NIKKI

When I woke up, the vapors of my drunken delirium were still haunting my head, making it ache like an SOB. Luckily, I didn't have class today which meant I could stay in bed all day and study for the last final of my junior year, which just happened to be tomorrow. That, and I could do my best to forget the fact that I'd come on to Derek last night.

Oh my God, I came on to Derek last night!

The words echoed through my sluggish mind, causing a nauseous feeling in the pit of my stomach. As soon as the thought occurred to me, Dani opened the door and walked in with a towel wrapped around her head and another one around her body.

"Good morning, sunshine. How's my little alky this morning?"

"Completely mortified, humiliated and embarrassed about what I did last night," I grumbled. "And it tastes like a dog just took a huge shit in my mouth."

"Well, don't get too close to me then!" She smiled as she turned to her bed and started dressing in the outfit she'd laid out for herself.

"Ha ha," I muttered as I berated myself for being such a total and complete idiot. "I can't believe I came onto him last night and he pushed me away! How am I ever going to face him again?" My attention fixed on the dark brown carpet in our bedroom. "I can't believe I did that."

"You're going to face him just like you always do," Dani answered as she pulled on her skinny jeans and smiled at me. "You're going to act like nothing happened."

I frowned because that just sounded so completely stupid. "How am I going to pretend it didn't happen?"

"You know how to pretend, silly," she answered matter-of-factly. "I did you a favor and skimmed through our *Femme Fatale Handbook* to see if there might be a section on emergencies, and guess what?"

"What?"

"There is! So, I read it, and guess what it said?"

"What?"

"What I just told you," she answered with a smug smile. "Jane said that *not* all hope is lost and you just have to pick up right where you left off. You treat him the same way you were treating him and, above all, you maintain your self-confidence. You just act like you're the one who had the change of heart. Like last night, that wasn't you at all."

"That's easier said than done."

"Yes, I'm sure it is, but it doesn't change the fact that you need to stay the course. Luckily for you, you can use the fact that you were drunk off your ass as an excuse."

"Everyone knows that's not an excuse."

"Well, it's *your* excuse and you're going to run with it."

"And what happens if there was too much damage done? What does Jane say then?"

"Then you take it as a lesson and you move on," Dani answered as she pulled out her plastic basket of toiletries and put on her Lady Speed Stick. "First things first, you have to forgive yourself and recognize that you're human and you're bound to make mistakes. Yes, the horse bucked you off, but you're going to get right back up on it, and you're going to take better control of those reins this time."

"I don't know how I can ever face him again, I'm so mortified and embarrassed and whatever other words there are for how I feel." I shook my head and felt like crying all over again. "And it's not like he's going to just sweep it under the rug, either."

"How do you know he won't?"

"Because he's Derek, and he looks for any opportunity to make me uncomfortable. It's like he gets some sick pleasure out of making me squirm."

"Well, if he does, then you laugh right along with him, like you don't think it's a big deal at all and it was all part of being happily drunk. Don't play the part of the sad and miserable sap who can't forgive herself. That's showing weakness, remember?"

"Yes." I nodded because I knew she was right.

"Instead, you just act like it was no big deal and you can't even remember what you did and it doesn't matter anyway because you're a femme fatale and you're hot and you can have anyone you damn well please."

"Except for my professor."

She frowned at me. "You can have him too—you just need to work a little harder for it."

"Blah."

She raised her brows at me. "You'll get over

this soon, Nikki. It's really nowhere near the big deal you're making it out to be." Then she smiled. "And on that note, I'm headed to class for my last final of the year!" Walking toward me, she gave me a quick peck on the top of my head. "If I don't talk to you before you talk to Derek, good luck." Then she gave me a salute like she thought she was a soldier or something.

"Thanks, Dani, and good luck on your final," I muttered as she grabbed her backpack, slung it over her shoulder and started for the door.

It was maybe an hour later that Derek texted me, asking me to meet him at his office.

As soon as I received the text, I got a sinking feeling, but reminded myself of Dani's words of wisdom and figured I better buck up. No, it wasn't going to be easy to face him, but if I wanted to be a femme fatale, and I still did, I had to forgive myself and move on. I'd act like it wasn't a big deal and I was over it and he should be too. End of story.

So, I got up, showered and, even though I wasn't feeling it, I dressed myself up in a brown miniskirt and a tight pink T-shirt which I paired with my heeled brown flip-flops. I left my hair down and applied just a bit of makeup. Once I was happy with my reflection, I grabbed my purse and a notebook and started the fifteen-minute walk to Derek's office.

My mind was a mess of thoughts on the way there, and a few times I had to talk myself out of turning around and returning to the shelter of my bedroom.

No, I'd be strong and I'd face Derek and act like nothing had happened last night. A tall order to be sure, but it was important I do this for my own sense of self-esteem. Otherwise, I wasn't sure how I could continue with my femme-fatale training and the truth was, I didn't want to stop.

When I reached the stairs leading up to the professors' offices, it felt like I was treading quicksand. But I took a deep breath and forced myself forward, eventually coming to stand in front of Derek's closed door. I was just about to knock when I heard his voice from the other side of the door, telling me to come in. Apparently, he must have heard my boots on the hardwood floors.

With my heart in my throat, I dutifully turned the doorknob and pushed the door in as I noticed Derek sitting behind his desk. He was leaning into his swivel chair with his long legs on top of his desk, his ankles crossed, like he was as comfortable and casual as it was possible to be. Well, good for him—at least one of us felt that way.

"Hi," I said with the most self-assured smile I could muster, my heart pounding through me as I turned to close the door.

"Nikki," he responded with an amused smile. "How's your head?"

"My head?"

"Yeah, after how drunk you were last night, I figured you'd have a hangover from hell."

"Oh, that." Even though my heart was pounding a mile a minute, I forced myself to laugh, like the whole thing was one, silly, little, inconsequential joke. Even if it wasn't.

"Yeah, that." I'd known Derek wouldn't let me live this one down and here was my proof.

"My head's fine. I mean, I'm tired, but I took enough Advil to sink a small ship." Then I smiled at him warmly as I helped myself to the chair directly across from him and put my purse down on the floor. I kept my notebook in my lap. "How are you?"

"I'm good." He eyed me speculatively.

"So, what's on for today?" I leaned forward and tried to appear excited, even if I felt like I was going to barf because my nerves were beyond frayed. "Are we going to review the curriculum for each class?"

His eyes narrowed as he studied me. Then he pyramided his fingers together in front of him and started bouncing them against each other, one by one. "Don't you think we need to have a talk first?"

My heart thumped and then went into overdrive. "A talk about what?" I was playing the part of innocent pretty damned well, if I had to say so myself.

"About what?" He gave me a skeptical laugh. "Um... about what happened last night."

"Did something happen last night?" I offered him another innocent smile like I had no idea what he was talking about and everything in my world was rainbows and unicorns.

"I'd say something definitely happened last night," he answered as he dropped his legs to the floor and sat up straight in his chair, before leaning forward.

"What are you talking about?"

"You kissed me."

"Did I?" I feigned a yawn as I cocked my head to the side. "I seem to recall, and gratnted my memory is a little foggy, but I thought you kissed me."

He chuckled. "I forget who kissed whom."

"Then it must never have happened at all."

He chuckled harder. "It happened alright."

"Hmm, then it must not have been that memorable because I can't say I remember much at all about last night." Then I smiled at him again. Somehow, and I had no idea how, but I was channeling someone smart, playful and confident, and she was doing a damned good job of throwing Derek off his game. Thank God for possession.

He stood up, immediately running one of his hands through his hair. Then he came around the desk, sat on the edge of it, maybe a foot or so away from me, and studied me for a good two seconds.

"So... we're good then?" He eyed me narrowly. "Nothing weird is going on?"

I shrugged. "We've always been good, Derek, no reason to stop being good now." The words spilled out of my mouth as if they had a life of their own, and inside I was doing the victory dance because I'd never imagined in a million years that I could have sounded as collected and unconcerned as I did.

He chuckled again as he stood up and then, gripping either armrest of my chair, he leaned down until our faces were mere inches apart. It was all I could do to continue breathing normally because he was close enough to kiss me—again.

"Good, because I'd hate for our working relationship to become muddled due to our sexual attraction to each other."

And that was when I realized what I needed to do. He was challenging me. By saying what he just had and by looming over me, he was showing me the powerful position he believed he held. He was using his physical size to intimidate me, but it wasn't going to work. I had to make sure it didn't work, anyway.

I didn't say anything as I leaned forward to place my notebook on top of his desk, and then I pushed him away as I stood up. He took a step back as he, too, stood but still, only a few inches of air separated us. Of course, I had to look up at him because he was so much taller than I was, but I didn't care—just in refusing to stay seated, and in refusing to let him loom over me like he was some kind of god, I was illustrating the fact that I wasn't going to let him boss me around.

"Our sexual attraction to each other?" I repeated with a salacious smile as I stared into his eyes, refusing to look away. "Whoever said we had that? At least on my side …"

He smiled back at me and the pupils of his eyes dilated in a way that hinted at his sexual excitement. Well, at least that's what Dani had told me a few months ago—that pupil dilation was a surefire signal that a guy was interested in a woman. And Derek's pupils were definitely dilating.

"No one has to say it," he nearly whispered as he held my gaze, neither one of us willing to cede the other victory. "It's obvious."

My eyebrows reached for the ceiling. "Maybe to you it is." I cocked my head to the side as I continued to smile up at him, allowing my expression to completely contradict my words.

"But I can't say the same goes for me."

"Really?" He laughed, shaking his head. "You were pretty convincing last night."

I shrugged as I leaned forward and whispered into his ear: "Beer goggles, or in my case, Vodka goggles. Apparently, it's a condition that affects everyone."

"Oh, is that what that was?" he stared at me, a smirk still riding his lips. He was so close to me, and his eyes were burning with that desire I'd seen in them the night before—so much that I wasn't sure if he might try to kiss me. "Because it didn't feel that way to me."

"Of course, it was, Derek." I needed to put some distance between us, because there was no way I was going to allow him to kiss me. Not when I needed to play the part of aloof—because if he kissed me, I'd be spaghetti in his hands. And femme-fatales weren't spaghetti in a man's hands. I took my seat again and primly folded my hands in my lap as I smiled up at him, comfortable in the fact that *I* had been the one to break our proximity. "What else could it be?" He frowned down at me. "I mean, you're my professor and I'm your student … your *undergraduate* student."

"I *was* your professor," he corrected me as he leaned down above me again, returning his hands to either side of my chair. Apparently, he liked this position. One thing I did know, though, was that he was turned on. I could tell by the expression in his eyes and the way he couldn't seem to stomach any distance between us.

"And just for the record," he continued. "There's nothing stating that a professor can't date a student, *even an undergraduate one*, as long as there isn't a conflict of interest."

"Hmm," I feigned interest in my nails. "So, you're telling me you want to date me, Derek?" Then I laughed, trying to make him feel like I was making fun of him.

"No," he answered immediately. "I was just pointing out the flaw in your argument."

"Well, just for the sake of argument, since you seem so inclined toward them, wouldn't you say my being your teaching assistant *is* a conflict of interest?" I started chewing on my bottom lip, wanting to draw his attention to my mouth—something which worked like a charm.

"I don't know." He seemed flustered.

I took a deep breath and continued to hold his gaze, still smiling and still acting like this whole thing was just an amusing conversation that didn't mean anything. "Well, in my humble opinion, I would say it *is* a conflict. And seeing as how we both value our 'working relationship,' as you called it, I think it would probably behoove us to keep our distance from one another." Then I reached forward and unfolded his fingers from around my chair before placing my palm flat on his chest and pushing him away from me.

There was a moment of complete surprise in his expression, but then he remembered himself and immediately covered his surprise with cool detachment. He stood up and returned to the opposite side of the desk, where he leaned back into his chair and considered me with interest.

"It's good to see you back to your levelheaded self," he said. I could detect a tone of disappointment in his voice though.

"Oh, my levelheaded self never left," I answered with a smirk.

SIX
DEREK

The tight, red dress hugged every curve of her body.

She was full and round in all the places a woman ought to be, but slender and toned as well. She was stunning. There was no other word for her, and it burned me to admit it. Especially after our little altercation this afternoon in my office.

I'd never expected her to play disinterested like she had. Instead, I'd thought for sure she would have apologized a million times and worried whether or not I was still going to consider her for the position of T.A.

Instead, she'd kicked me on my ass, and I hadn't been able to pull my mind off her for the rest of the day. Every time I remembered how expertly she'd played her part, I couldn't help but smile. There was something about her that was getting under my skin. Actually, the truth was she'd already gotten under my skin, and now I wanted nothing more than to have her, to claim her. I wanted to take what was mine to take. Because Nikki needed to be mine. I wanted her, and I was the type of man who took what he wanted.

And as soon as you sleep with her, you'll lose interest in her—just like you do with every other woman you get involved with, I reminded myself. *No, it's better to keep her at arm's length so you can maintain a good working relationship with her. Jack off thinking about her, but don't allow yourself to even think about doing anything more.*

Ugh, that fucking voice in the back of my head that always had a point. That fucking voice that was always right. That fucking voice that I couldn't ignore.

I wanted Nikki, yes. I could admit that much. But I could also admit that I couldn't have her. And that realization stung me like all the pitchforks from hell. But it was a decision I had to fully accept because it was the *only* decision.

So why in hell had I invited her to dinner

tonight? Of course, I'd pretended that I'd just wanted to discuss the upcoming classes she'd be assisting me with because we never did get a chance to discuss them earlier, but that wasn't really the reason I'd asked her out. The real reason was because I wanted to see her. Simple as that.

"So, when are you going to dress the part of a nerdy teacher's assistant?" I asked as I eyed her with a faux-concerned expression. I'd just picked her up and seen to it that she was comfortably seated in the Bronco. And, of course, I'd noticed how her short dress rode up her thighs, barely covering her panties, if she was even wearing any. Truth was that I'd already checked her ass out as she'd gotten into the Bronco and I hadn't noticed any panty lines.

At the thought that the little vixen might not have been wearing panties, I wanted to force her legs apart and stick my head between her thighs and lick her until she orgasmed all over my tongue.

"When are you going to come to terms with the fact that your T.A. just happens to be innately sexy and there's nothing she can do about it?" she responded, completely unfazed by my question. It seemed like whenever I tried to throw her off, she required no recovery. She eyed me with one eyebrow drawn in an unimpressed sort of way.

God, this woman drove me fucking crazy.

"I'll admit that it's taking some getting used

to," I grumbled as I put the Bronco into drive and pulled into the street. It was true—my 'relationship' with Nikki, or whatever the hell you wanted to call this, was starting to aggravate me. I'd never had such an awkward friendship with a woman before. I wanted her so fucking badly I could taste it. And I'd basically admitted as much to her this afternoon. But I couldn't have her—because she was right—there was a line in the sand because she was my assistant. Not only that, but I also didn't want to upset the current level of respect I had for her. And I knew, based on every other experience I'd ever had with a woman, that once we had sex, she'd get attached and I'd want to run for cover. And that would be a shame the proportions of which I didn't even want to consider. So, no, I'd have to continue being her friend and her boss, and I'd have to continue talking my cock down, and I'd have to continue masturbating everyday while thinking about bending her over.

Fuck me, right?

No, dickhead, I reminded myself, *in the long run, it will be much better to maintain this frustrating friendship and keep her at arm's length. So, control your raging hard-on and think about orphans in Uganda or dog shit or something!*

So why was I still having this conversation with myself … repeatedly? Why was I still trying to talk myself out of dating her?

"Where are we going?" she asked as she glanced over at me, armed with her notebook, as usual. God, she was such a nerd. And somehow her nerdiness made me want her even more.

You've got it bad, I said to myself, frustrated and irritated by the thought. *Hmm, maybe it would be better to have sex with her even if it ruined everything?* It just came down to the fact that I wasn't sure how much longer I could last, feeling like I wanted to rip her fucking clothes off and shove myself inside her while demanding she tell me she was all mine.

Force her to tell you she's all yours? I scoffed at myself. *Goddamn, dude, what the hell is wrong with you?*

"There's a new Italian place in town I wanted to try," I answered gruffly because I was waging a full-on, internal war with myself. When we came to a red light, I found myself looking at her hungrily. She was just so damned easy to look at! As soon as I took in her cleavage and that confidently sexy expression on her face, my jeans started to feel tight in the crotch ... again. Son of a...

Am I really getting hard just by looking at her? I chastised myself. *Jesus, man, get ahold of yourself! You're forty, not eighteen!*

"You mean Giuseppe's?" she asked, frowning.

"Yeah, that's the one." I couldn't help but be

concerned because she didn't exactly look happy to be going there. "Why, you don't like it?" Had some other guy had the pleasure of taking her to Giuseppe's? And, if so, who could the asshole be… Not Beau Dickhead?

"No, it's not that I don't like it." She appeared to be searching for the right words. "I've never been there so I wouldn't know. It's just that it's …"

"What?" I demanded when she grew quiet. "It's what?"

"It's just expensive!"

I shrugged as if the expense wasn't such a big deal. Of course, being on a professor's salary, it *was* a big deal, but I didn't care how much our meal cost me. "Who cares about all that?" I smiled at her, relieved to know some other shmuck hadn't already taken her there. "You gotta play with the big dogs more often, Nik!"

"Oh, and you're one of the big dogs then?" She frowned at me.

"The biggest."

"Oh, my God, the hubris of this man!" Then she exhaled a long breath and did her best to hide her smile. "Just don't start getting any romantic thoughts in that man brain of yours," she continued as she turned to face me, her gaze resting on my hair. "You need a haircut." She then reached over and curled a piece of my hair at the nape of my neck around her finger.

"Thanks for noticing." She pulled her hand away and I sorely wished she'd leave it there, because I wanted to feel her fingers against the sensitive skin of my neck.

"No problem." She gave me a smile. "Just don't want your future students mistaking you for a homeless person."

I laughed in spite of myself before I remembered the conversation she'd abandoned a little while ago. "And, pray tell, just what romantic thoughts were you worried I was getting, by the way?"

"Oh, I don't know ... silly and romantic thoughts about you and me." She speared me with a pointed and challenging gaze.

I frowned at her. "Haven't we been through this already?"

She shrugged. "Maybe, but it appears one of us hasn't gotten the message through his very thick skull." Then she glanced at my hair again, reaching out to run it through her fingers. Every time she touched me, my skin broke out in goose bumps. "Maybe all that hair is getting in the way of your ears and, thus, affecting your auditory processing."

"Ha ha. Not funny." Then I looked at that smile she was wearing and instantly wished I hadn't. "And as for getting romantic thoughts about you, I'm not, so don't worry."

"Okay, just warning you." She shrugged as she

rolled her eyes.

"You don't believe me."

She feigned surprise. "I didn't say that."

"Then why are you rolling your eyes?"

"Was I rolling my eyes?"

"You were."

"Oh, probably just an errant speck of dust in one of them, that's all." Then she reached over and patted my thigh. "Not to worry, Casanova, your secret is safe with me."

"My secret?" I pulled into the parking lot of Giuseppe's. The attendant was suddenly in front of my door, and I felt myself suck in a mouthful of air in response. "Jesus, they're fucking prompt."

"Sounds like you've got a burr under your saddle." Then she laughed as the man opened my door and I unbuckled my seat belt, stepping down onto the asphalt below. When I walked around the Bronco in order to open Nikki's door, I found her already standing in front of me.

"I would have gotten the door for you," I said, annoyed another man had.

She smiled up at me sweetly but I knew better—there was nothing sweet in her eyes—the expression there was all victory. "You don't need to do that. We're just friends, remember?"

"Will you stop doing that?"

"Stop what?"

"Acting like I can't do nice things for you

because we're friends and we aren't friends."

"We aren't?"

"No, I'm your employer."

She shrugged. "Regardless of what we are, it doesn't change the fact that I'm a strong, independent woman of the twenty-first century, Derek, and I can open my own door. Didn't you learn anything in our *Feminist Literature* course?"

"You're going to give me a nervous tic," I grumbled as I insisted on opening the door to the restaurant for her and she walked inside. I bypassed her and approached the hostess, letting her know I had a reservation. The attractive brunette checked her list and, finding my reservation, she grabbed two menus before escorting us through the ten or so tables in the small room, each covered with a white tablecloth.

I couldn't help but notice the heads turning to watch Nikki as she gracefully walked through the dining room. By the way she looked straight ahead, I didn't think she was even aware that most the men in the room were giving themselves whiplash just trying to sneak a glance at her.

The hostess showed us to our table, handed us our menus, and then laid Nikki's white napkin across her lap before replacing mine with a black one to match my black pants.

"Fancy," Nikki said as soon as the woman walked away.

"So, what was this secret of mine that you were talking about?" I demanded, intent on knowing what the hell was going on in that fucking sexy as hell head of hers.

"Secret?" She shook her head, like she couldn't remember what conversation I was talking about. She was going to drive me to complete insanity.

"Yeah, you said you would keep my secret safe."

Then she was quiet for a few minutes as she brought her hand to her mouth and chewed on her lip while she, ostensibly, tried to figure out what I was talking about. "I can't remember saying that," she said finally with a dismissive shrug. "So, I have no idea what I was talking about." Then she glanced down at my menu which I was holding in front of me. "What are you going to order?"

I wasn't paying attention to my menu, though. Instead, I couldn't pull my gaze away from her. There was something about her … God, I didn't even know what it was. Yes, she was hot, gorgeous, beautiful, whatever word you wanted to call her. But I'd been with women who were equally pretty or maybe even prettier. Yet, Nikki was unlike any other woman I'd ever met, and it was driving me nuts that I couldn't figure out why.

I have to have her, the words blared through my mind and I had to forcefully push them back. The moment the thought entered my head though, I started to panic. I felt like I was relinquishing control, like I was caving. And it wasn't a feeling that caused me any level of comfort. I didn't want a relationship—I never had. Not with Nikki, not with any woman. I was convinced that I wanted to be a bachelor for a very long time. So why did I…

You want to have lots of sex with lots of women, I reminded myself. *So, snap yourself the fuck out of it and stop lusting after her! Put her firmly in the employee category and stop thinking about what she feels like between her thighs. Stop thinking about how tight and wet you know she'll be. Stop thinking about thrusting yourself so far inside her that she screams. Stop thinking about her choking on your length.*

I forced my attention back to my menu, but I couldn't seem to concentrate on reading any of it. Instead, my mind kept floating back to images of Nikki naked on my bed, looking up at me with those sensual eyes of hers while I thrust inside of her again and again.

"Earth to Derek," she said, suddenly pulling me away from my lustful thoughts.

"What?"

She motioned to the waiter who somehow had appeared next to our table without my ever spotting him. It was as if the air had just spat him out.

"Do you know what you want?" Nikki continued, prodding me to speak.

"Oh," I glanced back at my menu, feeling suddenly embarrassed that I was so clearly off my game.

"He's a little slow," Nikki said to the man, sounding like she was apologizing. "Probably need to give him some more time. That, and English is his second language."

"English is not my second language!" I demanded, a smile already taking my lips. "But my dining partner here has a smart mouth."

The waiter nodded but looked completely uncomfortable, like he had no idea how to react to us. "Very good, sir," he finally said.

"Nik, do you know what you want?"

"Yes, my darling," she answered, throwing me completely for a loop. "I'd like the salmon, please." She faced the waiter and he dutifully wrote her order down. "And I would love it if my husband over here would stop spending so much time with my best friend."

I felt my stomach drop as I glanced at her and caught her huge smile. The waiter, meanwhile, said nothing but kept his gaze strictly glued to his notebook. So, the little minx wanted to play, did she? Well, then, we would play.

"If my dear wife would stop running up the credit cards and saying she has a headache every night, maybe I wouldn't *need* to spend so much time with her best friend." I faced Nikki with placid smile. Her eyes were wide and she was doing her best to hide a giggle which she turned into a cough. I glanced back at my menu before looking up at our waiter, who was now a very pronounced shade of red. "And I will have the filet, please. Medium rare."

"And your side, sir?" he asked, as if Nikki's and my conversation were nothing out of the ordinary.

I glanced over at Nikki and found she was still wearing a huge smile. "Brussel sprouts," I answered as I closed my menu and handed it to him. "Because those are Jill's favorite."

"I should just stand up and walk out of here right now," Nikki answered, her voice wavering as she did her best to conceal her smile.

"I will be back to check on you both when your food arrives," the poor waiter announced as he nodded quickly and then hightailed it out of the room.

As soon as he left, Nikki exploded into a round of giggles and I couldn't do much to keep from laughing either.

"We are going straight to hell for that," I said as I shook my head.

"But wasn't it fun?" There was a mischievous twinkle in her eye.

"Too much fun," I answered as the words echoed in my mind.

SEVEN
The Femme Fatale Handbook
Chapter Ten: Make Him Need You

In this chapter, we will discuss the fact that you have to make your target think he needs you, that he can't live without you.

You have to make him equate you with his own sense of happiness. Play on the fact that every man feels like there's a part of his life that's lacking. Of course, he will probably never admit this to you, but it's true nonetheless. People wear masks around other people in an attempt to make it seem as though they're completely happy with their lives. Think about Facebook. The difference between someone's real life and the life they pretend to have on Facebook are usually night and day.

The truth of the matter is that it's impossible to be one-hundred percent satisfied with one's life—it goes against the laws of human nature. Humans are never happy with what they have. They are, instead, forever reaching, looking for something, wanting whatever it is they don't have, and they are never satisfied. He might think he's happy and content with his life, but you need to show him that he isn't. You must stir a need within him. You must make him aware of an emptiness in his life and then position yourself as the antidote to that emptiness. Make him feel like you're the one thing that can make him feel whole again. You're the one thing that can relieve him of his boredom or cure him of his loneliness.

*Not sure what it is that he's lacking in his life? Look at his personality and pinpoint his insecurities. Every man has them. Let me repeat that—**every man has insecurities!** Some just do a better job of covering them up. It's your duty to uncover them. Any of his insecurities are fair game. Find them, and once you do, focus on* *them—make them seem bigger than they really are and then project yourself as the solution to whatever problem he has. Present yourself as the answer to his lack of excitement or adventure. You're a break from the norm. You're the drug, and you must make him become dependent on you.*

###
NIKKI

"So, how's it going?" Dani asked as we jogged through Meadow Lane Park which was just down the street from sorority row.

"It's going really well," I answered truthfully but then sighed, something which wasn't easy given the pace we were keeping. I started to slow down to a walk as Dani followed suit beside me. "Well, it is and it isn't."

"What do you mean?"

"I mean that I think it's working on Derek's side. He can't seem to take his eyes off me, and he seems to look for any excuse to hang out with me."

"Okay," Dani started, looking at me with confusion. "Both of which sound like they should be categorized in the good column? Am I missing something?"

I nodded. "Yes, you're missing the fact that *I'm* totally falling for *him*."

She started to shake her head. "You can't do

that."

"I know, Dani, that's my point." I sounded annoyed because she was just affirming what I already knew. "But it's not exactly easy to stop myself, is it?"

"You have to!" She faced me with an earnest expression. "You can't lose control, Nikki. Not when you've gotten this far with him—you're almost there—almost about to prove that all this Jane stuff is true."

I nodded as I took a deep breath. "So how do you talk yourself out of having feelings for someone?"

"You focus on all the ways he's not good for you. You keep telling yourself as many times as you need to that you aren't falling for him, but that he's falling for you. You tell yourself to keep your cool. You remind yourself that you're a femme fatale and you want to stay that way." She took a deep breath. "You tell yourself that you're the one who is in charge and in control and that he's nothing more than your target, your victim."

"Maybe," I answered with a quick nod. "I guess that's all I can do." Then I faced her as I stretched my arms up above my head. "Because I don't know what else to do."

"You nearly threw your game that night when you got drunk and you came on to him," Dani reminded me, her tone dead serious. "But luckily you followed Jane's advice and you were able to get back up on the horse after it bucked you off. And it seems like you were even able to use what could have been a really bad situation to your advantage. You don't want to throw all of that away, Nik."

"He calls me Nik now." I started shaking my head because I knew I shouldn't have felt giddy over that fact, but I did. The truth was, where Derek was concerned, I was in deep and I didn't know if it was even possible to get myself back to the surface again.

"Who cares?" Dani demanded. "Who cares what the hell he calls you? Don't get in over your head—not until he offers you what you want."

"What do you mean?"

"Well, what do you want from him?"

I shrugged as I thought about it. "A relationship, I guess?"

"Okay, so until he offers you a relationship, you continue to play the game." Then she started shaking her head. "I'm not sure a relationship between you both is even a good idea."

"Why not?"

"Don't me wrong, I really like Derek, but I'm not sure he's someone you should get attached to. He just doesn't strike me as boyfriend material."

"Why?"

"Why?" she repeated, shaking her head and

shrugging. "Because he's a playboy! You told me yourself that's exactly what he is."

"Right." I swallowed hard.

"Not to mention all the rumors about him. I'm just... I'm just worried that Derek isn't someone who will ever settle down, or at least not for a long time. I mean—he's forty and he's never been married?"

I nodded. "Good point."

"I'm thinking he's good at breaking hearts, Nik, not making them."

"Dude, you should work for Hallmark."

"I'm serious."

"I know you are, and I also know you're right." I breathed in deeply and then shook my head. "Which doesn't help the fact that my dumbass heart still is crushing on him bad."

"Think about his reputation. Think about all the girls he's banged and then left them on their sorry asses. Do you want to be one of those?"

"No," I answered honestly. "I definitely don't want to be banged and left behind on my sorry ass."

"So stop letting yourself get carried away with romantic feelings you have no business feeling. Pull an overnighter reading *The Femme Fatale Handbook* if you need to beef up your defenses."

I cocked my head to the side as I considered it. "Not a bad idea, actually."

"You're in the home stretch, girly," Dani continued with a big nod. "As I see it, you're going to have Derek eating out of your hand pretty soon."

"To what end though?" I sighed.

"What do you mean?"

"If he's eating out my hand, doesn't that mean he wants a relationship with me?"

"Maybe, maybe not." She looked at me as if she failed to see my point.

"So, if he's eating out of my hand, wouldn't that mean that I won?"

She started shaking her head. "No. You win when you continue to play him, when you continue to hold the strings."

"Cleopatra got into two long-term relationships all while still pulling the strings."

"Okay, good point," Dani ceded. "But you're not Cleopatra."

"Ugh." Still, I couldn't argue with her because I wasn't Cleopatra and so far, my track record of 0/2 wasn't looking so hot.

"You're still in training," Dani continued. "And you've got a long way to go still, Nik. So keep your legs shut tight and don't let Derek's penis between them."

"You have such a way with words." Even though I smiled at her, I didn't really feel it.

###

I knew Dani was right.

Everything she'd said was on point.

And even though I also was fairly convinced that I could wrap Derek around my finger if I wanted to, I couldn't say that feeling brought me any sort of warmth. The truth was that I liked him—like *really* liked him. We had so much fun together and he made me laugh. And he was hot. Insanely hot. And I totally wanted to have sex with him. Like more than I could remember ever wanting to have sex with any guy ever.

And the fact that I couldn't was bumming me out. But Dani was right—I didn't want to sleep with Derek and wake up dumped the next morning. Because I did value our strange friendship or whatever it was. I valued our laughs and talks and our interactions with each other, and if that was all we were ever going to be, well, that would have to be good enough for me. It *was* good enough for me.

So why wasn't I texting him back? I glanced down at my phone as I lay in my bed and sighed. His last text stared back up at me.

Hello? You there?

I couldn't bring myself to respond. And it wasn't that I was playing some game, aka the part of the femme fatale who was ignoring him. I just didn't *want* to respond. I didn't want to because I didn't want to get my hopes up on Derek. I didn't want to get even more attached to him than I already was.

And what was more, I wanted him to stop pursuing me because his constant attention was making this whole situation even harder on me. The truth was that I wanted things to go back to how they'd been in the beginning—when I thought of him as nothing more than an egregious flirt—a time when I didn't take him seriously. I wanted to go back to a time before I'd seen inside him—into a part of him that he kept walled off. A part that was kind and sweet. The part of him that had caused him to put his arm around me when we'd walked past Brandon. It was much easier dealing with Derek when I thought he was just one dimensional.

So, I didn't text him back.

And I didn't answer his texts or his phone call the next day or his multiple texts and phone calls the day after. So, I shouldn't have been too surprised when he came by the ZTS house the following day.

I was sitting in my room, watching a cooking show and waiting for Dani to get back from getting her nails done. There was a knock on my door, and when I opened it, I found a very pissed off Derek standing there, staring at me.

"You better be dead," he started as he glared at

me. "Or, at the very least, maimed to the point of near death." He looked me up and down. "But you appear to be neither."

I laughed because I couldn't help it. "Yeah, I'm not dead."

"I can see that." He pushed the door open and stepped into my room, taking stock of it quickly before he closed the door behind him and faced me with anger written all over his face.

"Apparently you aren't very familiar with sorority houses," I started.

"I'm very familiar with them as I've spent a lot of time in various sorority rooms," he answered, his tone like ice.

His response didn't faze me. He was angry and he was lashing out at me. That much was obvious. "Hmm, well, I find that hard to believe, because if you *were* familiar with sorority houses, you'd realize we have a rule where we aren't allowed to have guys in our rooms."

He waved me away with an unconcerned hand. "That is an outdated and stupid rule which I guarantee you every girl in this house has broken … repeatedly. And... what's more... I'm not just some random guy."

"Explain that to the house mom."

"What's going on with you?" he demanded, clearly getting to the point of why he'd come. "You've been ignoring me for three days."

"I've just been busy." I dropped my attention to the hemline of my sweater and pretended extreme interest in it.

"Busy doing what?" He took a step closer and I took one back.

"Oh, you know..." I shrugged and lost my nerve because the way he was looking at me—it was like he couldn't make up his mind whether he wanted to yell at me or kiss me. I immediately looked away.

"No, I don't know." I made the mistake of looking up at him and found him staring at me with his arms crossed and an angry expression on his face. As soon as our eyes met, I swallowed hard.

"I've, uh," I started but found the words failing me.

"You realize summer classes start in four days, right?"

I nodded.

"And we haven't reviewed all the lesson plans in their entirety."

"I figured we could review them as we go. I mean, we've already gone over all the information for the first two weeks."

He didn't respond right away but stared at me, his mouth drawn into a tight line. "Are you seeing someone?"

I frowned, completely thrown off by the question. "Um, what?"

He took a step closer to me and I felt my heartbeat start to race in my chest. "Are you dating someone?" Then he took a deep breath and shook his head. "I was trying to figure out why the hell you'd completely stop talking to me, and that was the only reason I could come up with."

"I don't know what that has to do—"

"Is some guy telling you we can't be friends or something?" His tone was suddenly angrier as if the thought was sending him into a fit.

"I thought we weren't friends?"

His eyes narrowed. "Answer the goddamned question, Nikki."

"No, I'm not seeing anyone."

"Then why the fuck aren't you texting me back?" He took another step closer to me so no more than a few inches of air now separated us. By now my heart was pounding and I couldn't look him in the face.

"Um," I started.

"Look at me." He reached forward and tipped my chin up, holding my face so I couldn't drop my attention. "Why did you go silent on me?"

"I, uh, I don't know." I swallowed hard.

"You don't know?" He laughed but the sound wasn't happy. "What does that even mean?" Then he shook his head and dropped his hands back to his side. I immediately dropped my gaze to the ground but then forced it back to his face. And that was where I made my mistake.

He was beautiful. His dark eyes were so full of anger and hurt that I wanted nothing more than to reach out to him and run my fingers down the side of his face and tell him how I really felt about him. But I knew I couldn't do that.

"I," I started and then took a deep breath, trying to still my heart.

But I wasn't able to finish my sentence. In one fluid motion, he bridged the distance separating us, gripped the back of my head, and brought his mouth down on mine. I was shocked for maybe a split second before all my repressed feelings started flooding me and I felt myself melting into him. I wrapped my arms around his neck and pushed myself into him, opening my mouth so I could feel and taste his tongue. He groaned as he gripped me around the waist and pulled me into him, even closer. So close that I could feel his erection pressing into my waist. And then thoughts of him naked, of me naked, began swarming my head like an upset hornet's nest. I could imagine him thrusting into me, feeling my wetness. I could imagine looking into his eyes as he took me. God, I wanted him. I wanted him so badly, it hurt.

"No!" I insisted as soon as the thought of where this was headed raced into my head. I pulled away from him and then placed my palms against his chest, pushing him away another few inches.

"We can't do this."

"You want this as much as I do," he insisted. I couldn't answer because I was panting. I did want him. God, I wanted him more than I'd ever wanted anyone. But I couldn't give in to these feelings, because I didn't want to end up dumped.

Again.

EIGHT
The Femme Fatale Handbook
Chapter Eleven: The Subject of Sex

Let's talk about sex! I don't know about you, but this is one of my favorite subjects!

This is an important subject, so pay close attention and reread this section however many times you need to in order to make sure all this information sinks in.

So getting down to the rules about sex

*regarding men and women ... They go something like this: Before a woman sleeps with a man, she has all the power. Afterward, **he** has all the power.*

Repeat. That. To. Yourself.

Over and over and over again. Repeat it as many times as it takes you to fully understand before you give up the va-jay-jay. I know it isn't fair and I know you're angry about it. And I'm sure you're wondering why it has to be that way. So, I'm going to tell you ...

In general, men want sex and women want a commitment. That's not to say men don't want commitment, sometimes they do, and I would say that most men are happiest when they are in a good relationship. But I can also promise you that commitment isn't the driving force behind a man's behavior when it comes to women; sex is. Blame it on biology if you need to, but the fact remains. Men want sex! And they will take sex pretty much from whoever is willing to give it to them.

So how do you know when it's the right time to surrender the booty? This is an important question! Keep in mind that no woman has ever lost interest in a man because he slept with her on the first date, while men lose interest in women all the time for the same thing. Yes, it's a double standard; yes, it's unfair; yes, it sucks, but it is what it is, so rather than fighting it, use this knowledge to your advantage!

Just how will you use it to your advantage? First, you must understand what constitutes the right time to get intimate with a man. The answer to this complex question is fairly simple. It's not about waiting three dates or six dates or whatever Cosmo *magazine is telling you. When it comes to having sex with a man, the number of dates doesn't matter—it's an arbitrary measure that really tells you nothing. It doesn't matter! Yes, you heard that correctly—the number of dates you wait before you have sex with a man is unimportant! What matters is the **quality** of the time you spend together.*

Think about it like this—let's say you don't have sex with a guy before date three and you tell him as much, thinking it makes you look somehow more selective or like you care about yourself more than just giving it up on date one. In a guy's mind, though, he doesn't read it like that. Instead, he thinks to himself, OK, I just have to take her out three times and then I'm in like Flynn! He's not going to think any more of you because you make him wait three days, because three days doesn't mean anything to him.

The question you need to ask yourself is whether or not you've developed any sort of a real connection with him and whether he's developed a real connection to you. So, now you're wondering what I mean by a 'real connection', right? I think examples might help illustrate this point the best ...

Let's say a woman decides to have sex with a man on the first date after an evening of intense, meaningful conversation in which both the man and the woman feel very much interested and in tuned with one another. They feel close to each other. Rather than surface conversations about how many siblings he has and what his favorite color is, they talked about his career ambitions, his family, what he feels is lacking in his life, etcetera.

Through their intense conversation, they bonded with each other, they let one another in. This type of situation will be much more likely to lead to a relationship, even if the woman decides to have sex with the man on the first date (although I'm not saying you should sleep with him after date one—the longer you can wait, the better). The point is you're trying to get beyond the superficiality of first introductions so you can get to the meat of who this man is. And that's usually impossible to do after just meeting him once.

Now, take the same situation and let's say the surface conversation, though friendly and polite, lasted all night and then they had sex? I doubt he'd call her again. Why? Because they had nothing invested in each other, so all they really had was the sex. Sure, he might call her again if he gets bored or if the sex was really good and he wants another go. But this type of situation won't last long because he will think she's easy—that she'll give it up to the next guy who comes along just as easily as she gave it up to him.

The answer to this important question about sex is that the right time to have sex with a man is when he's shown a level of investment in you— when you have the power enough on your side that you know he's not just going to leave as soon as you both do the deed.

Keep in mind that men don't value what they perceive is readily and easily available to all other men. So, when you have sex with a guy before you really know him, it's easy for him to assume that you're doing the same thing with other men. And in the man brain, that's a big turn off. A man wants to know that he's worked hard for you, not that you offered yourself up to the first guy who came around showing interest.

So, to sum all this up into an easy to remember and convenient test for yourself: Before sleeping with a man, ask yourself: is he interested in you, or is he just interested in having sex with you? If you can't distinguish between the two, it's not time to have sex with him.

Girls, I want you to understand how men think about sex but I also want you to remember that a femme fatale does not have sex with a man until she's gotten what she wants from him!

Let me repeat that: A femme fatale doesn't have sex with a man until she's gotten what she wants from him. And sometimes you might be able to get what you want and move on without having sex with him at all! It all depends on what it is you're after. So, unless you've gotten that commitment, that gift, that money, that trip, etcetera, stay in the driver's seat!

###

DEREK

I knew I was making a mistake.

I knew I shouldn't have been doing what I was doing, and I knew I'd come to regret it. But I couldn't help myself. I reached for Nikki again, but she backed away, concern and worry in her features.

And fuck it all but my cock was so hard, it was hurting. Goddamnit, I wanted this woman and I wanted her like I'd never wanted anything else in my life. By this point, I was going to have her. Fuck my better judgement, fuck that fucking voice in the back of my head. Fuck any and everything that was going to get in my way.

"I don't understand," I said, feeling frustrated all the way down to my toes. "Why are you playing games with me?"

"I'm not," she started, but by the expression on her face, she wasn't telling the truth.

"You came on to me the other night, Nikki." I

could feel anger beginning to brew inside me because if there was one thing I couldn't respect, it was game playing and I had a feeling she was doing exactly that. "You wanted me and we both know you did." I paused. "And I was the one who said we couldn't."

"So why are you doing this now?" she insisted, fire beginning to burn in her eyes. And that fire in her eyes ignited my dominance even more. I wanted to throw her down on her bed, rip her clothes off and sink myself inside her just so I could show her who was in charge.

"You don't get it, do you?" I shook my head and laughed without humor. "I wanted you that night! I wanted you almost as much as I want you now, but I wasn't about to take advantage of you when you were as drunk as you were."

"Well..." She took a deep breath. "Thank you." She finally brought those beautiful, wide blue eyes up to mine, and I felt my own breath hitch. I couldn't remember ever finding a woman more beautiful than I found her now.

"So, why are you doing this, Nik?" My voice was now softer. "I don't understand you at all. If you want me and I want you, why are you doing this?"

"Because it's the right thing to do." She smiled at me almost wistfully. "You know who you are, Derek." The playfulness was completely missing from her voice now and there was an earnest expression in her eyes.

"And who am I?" I nearly interrupted her.

She cocked her head to the side as she appeared to ponder my question. Finally, she looked at me and her expression was vacant, like she was wearing a poker face. "You're a bachelor, a playboy. You're a rebel, a rake—there are a million titles for you. The point is: you love nothing more than the chase." I couldn't argue with her and swallowed hard, surprised by thtat realization. I was speechless, so she continued. "And I confuse you."

"Yes," I answered immediately, finally finding my tongue. "You do confuse me, and you frustrate me, and I've never wanted anything as badly as I want you."

She smiled almost sadly. "Because you want to conquer me, Derek." She gave a little shake of her head. "But what then? What happens *after* we have sex?" I didn't answer because I couldn't bring myself to say the words. "The same thing that happens with every other woman you fuck," she said softly. "And it's not worth it to me to take that chance, because I like you; I care about you and I care about our friendship. Even if you refuse to call it a friendship, that's what it is."

"So, this is what it feels like to be put in the friend category?" I gave her a laugh I didn't feel. I just... didn't know what else to say.

She laughed, and the sound of her voice made me want to grab her and pull her into my arms, just so I could feel her soft skin and smell her hair. God, I wanted to touch her, have her close to me. "I value and I respect you, Derek."

"But you don't believe that I value and respect you?" I was almost angry because I valued her more than I'd ever valued another woman before. And I respected her even more. It was impossible not to respect her because she was so smart, so driven, so funny, so sweet and kind.

"I do believe you respect me. Of course, I do. And I know you care about me, but you seem to be having a hard time limiting this situation of ours to just friendship or a working relationship— whatever you want to call it. The point is, I'm sure you can admit that it's the right thing to do."

"That's putting it mildly."

She laughed again, and even though I was beyond frustrated, to the point of being angry, I found myself smiling down at her.

"Do you have any female friends, Derek?" she asked as she eyed me pointedly. "And I don't mean girls you've slept with who are willing to take any attention from you they can get. I mean purely platonic friendships with women where you don't want to have sex with them and you never have."

"No," I answered immediately. "And I don't

feel that way towards you either, and I never will. Be disappointed in me all you want." I knew I sounded infantile and defensive, but there it was. "But I will always want to have sex with you." I shrugged. "I am but a man, after all."

She sighed, but there was a smile on her lips. "I understand that and I forgive you."

"Oh, you forgive me?" I quirked an eyebrow at her to show her I wasn't amused, even though I was.

"I do."

"Okay, Mother Theresa," I started as I crossed my arms against my chest and eyed her incredulously. "So, what happens now that we've both admitted to our sexual desire for one another and agreed that anything between us is a bad idea?"

She shrugged and raised both brows at me. "We agree to be friends. We make a pact not to come on to one another, and to respect each other as people." She took a breath. "I would love to be your friend, Derek, if you want to be mine?" Then she extended her hand and I looked at it with little interest.

I cleared my throat. "I don't want to be your friend."

"You know what will happen if we have sex," she insisted, frowning at me while she still held her hand extended.

"No, I don't know." I kept both of my arms

crossed against my chest. Yes, I was acting like a spoiled child and no, I didn't care.

She shook her head. "Well, I know. And I'm not willing to bet our friendship on it."

"So, it's not worth it to you to find out what we could be together?" I was growing angry and defensive again. This wasn't the response I'd expected when I'd come here. I'd fully expected her to admit she was dating someone and then I was going to do my best to make sure I fucked up whatever budding relationship she had so I could claim her for myself. But friendship hadn't been something I'd considered. Not at this point.

"I don't understand."

"What if we *are* right for each other?" I demanded, staring at her imploringly. "What if your fear is getting in the way of something that could be great?"

"Listen to what you're saying, Derek." Her voice was calm and smooth. It didn't seem like there was any emotion in her eyes at all. It seemed like this whole situation was much easier for her to accept than it was for me, and I couldn't say I liked that at all.

"I know what I'm saying."

She shook her head. "You're fighting just because you want to get your way, but everything you're saying goes completely counter to who and what you are."

"I hate it that you think you've got me figured out."

"I hate it that you keep denying your true nature. Accept who you are, and you'll find it's much easier to live your life."

"Aren't you supposed to be younger than me?" I insisted with a frown. She laughed as she nodded. "Well, start acting like it and stop talking like you're fucking Socrates or Plato."

We both were quiet for a few seconds as we looked at each other and her words started to sink in. She was right—she did know me, and everything she was saying was true—I was the eternal bachelor and even though I felt like I wanted a relationship with her, I was probably just kidding myself. It just sucked because I wasn't used to not getting what I wanted. And she was at the top of my list.

She was finally the one to break the silence. "So, are we good, Derek?"

I thought about it for a few seconds before I nodded and grabbed her, pulling her into my chest as I wrapped my arms around her and plopped my chin on top of her head. "Yeah, we're good, you fucking pain in my ass."

She glanced up at me and laughed before she put her head on my chest and held me even tighter.

NINE
NIKKI
One Week Later

I wasn't sure how I'd done it, but I'd managed to firmly put Derek into the friendship category.

And I'd given up on trying to seduce him. It just hadn't felt right. I respected him and I liked him too much to try to turn him into my puppy dog. No, I valued our friendship and our working relationship too much for that. So, I'd decided to focus my femme fatale attention on Beau instead.

Not because I wanted a relationship with him. Actually, I didn't want anything from him. I just figured he'd be a good candidate based on the fact that he'd already screwed me over once so I wasn't exactly sympathetic to his cause. And I figured if I could get him to eat out of my hand, that would be a pretty tall order, given our history. Yes, Beau would prove to be a challenge (not like Derek was a challenge), but a mini challenge and that was currently what I was after.

"Where are you headed tonight?" Dani asked as I took one last look at my reflection in the mirror to make sure I looked presentable.

"I have a date."

"Thanks for that, Captain Obvious." She frowned as she eyed me from where she was lying on her bed with one leg propped up over the other one. She was busily reading the notebook, and from what I could tell, she was nearly finished with it.

"My date is taking me to *The Greek House* for dinner," I answered as I gave her a quick smile.

"And would your date happen to be Beau?" There was another frown. She hadn't been silent about her dislike for Beau and the fact that she thought it was a horrible idea that I was 'dating' him. I wasn't sure when it had happened exactly, but Dani was now firmly in Derek's camp. She'd even gone so far as to take back all the things she'd said about him not being good boyfriend material. I wasn't sure what had gotten into her, but I was firmly convinced that not only was Derek terrible boyfriend material, but he was a bad bet in general. He just wasn't capable of having a relationship. Or that was what I kept telling myself.

"Yes, with Beau," I answered, to which she immediately stuck her tongue out and made a sound deep in her throat that hinted of disapproval.

"Okay, well, have fun." Her phone buzzed and she reached for it where it lay beside her. "Hello, handsome," she said to the phone with a huge grin as she texted back.

"And who are you so giddy about?"

She glanced up at me, her smile still in full effect. "Luke."

"Really?" The more I thought about it, the more I decided they'd make a great couple. Luke seemed like a very nice guy and he was also pretty shy which I liked. He hadn't made a move on her yet, according to Dani, and I thought that was exactly what she needed—a guy she could take things slowly with. Not to mention the fact that the two of them looked adorable together.

"Yes, really," she answered as she put the phone down. "I've decided to make Luke my target."

"Okay, that's a good idea. And have you decided what you want from him?"

"A relationship." Her expression was thoughtful. "I've decided that Luke pretty much ticks all the boxes on paper."

"That sounds like you're taking a very organized approach to your dating life."

She nodded. "I am, and I'm going about this whole seduction thing very carefully. Once I finish the notebook, I'm going to read it again, and then I'm going to plan out my attack."

"Remember to have fun with it." I started for the door. "And once he waves his white flag of surrender, give the guy a break."

"Maybe," she answered with a devilish smile. "Anyway, have fun with jerkface." I grabbed my purse from where it was hanging just beside the door. "I hope he chokes on his hummus and dies."

"Dani!" I said with a surprised laugh. "You know you shouldn't joke like that!"

"Blah." She gave me a look as she waved me out the door.

###

Dinner with Beau was enjoyable, but I was relieved when we were on the way back to the ZTS house.

Even though I could say I had a good time with him, it wasn't anywhere near as fun as the time I spent with Derek. Beau didn't make me laugh the way Derek did. I also found myself struggling to find subjects to talk about during dinner. We just didn't really have anything in common. It was strange, but I couldn't understand how in the world I'd ever found him interesting in the first place. And there was no way in hell I could imagine being in a relationship with him, so it sort of stunned me that I'd ever wanted one. Furthermore, I couldn't say my heart was in the idea of seducing him. Why? Because I didn't want to spend any more time with him.

When we pulled up in front of the house, Beau passed it and parked up the street a ways, underneath a tree and away from the glaring light of the overhead streetlamps. He killed the Dodge Ram's engine as he turned to face me with a big smile.

"I had a great time tonight," he said.

"I did too, thank you." I undid my seat belt and reached for my purse which was on the floor between my feet. Then I opened my door and hopped down onto the asphalt, not wanting to wait for him to come around and open the door for me. Truth be told, I was eager to get back to my room so I could crawl into bed and hopefully talk to Dani for a little while if she was still awake. I figured she'd be happy to know I wasn't at all attracted to Beau and was no longer interested in making him the target of my seduction. Who my target should be from this point on was a complete and total mystery to me, but I hoped I'd find one soon.

"It's cold out here," Beau said as he walked around the truck and stopped in front of me, taking a step forward as I took a step back, my butt pressing up against the truck. It was then that I realized just how huge this guy was. He towered over me by more than a head and was easily twice my width.

"Yeah, so I should probably get back to my room so you can get back into the truck so we both don't freeze out here." I gave him a tremulous laugh as I wrapped my arms around myself. It wasn't in response to the cold, though—more because I was uncomfortable. There was just something about Beau that made me feel ill-at-ease. I couldn't put my finger on it, though. Maybe I just didn't know him that well.

Beau nodded and appeared to be thinking about what I'd just said. "So, are you going to invite me up?" He sounded and looked hopeful.

I immediately felt myself frowning as a surge of offended anger began to bubble up inside me. Who the hell did he think he was? Just because we'd had sex once, he expected it again? "I hadn't planned on it." I answered honestly, no amount of apology in my tone.

"Really?" His eyebrows furrowed as he looked completely surprised. "I gotta admit I didn't expect you to say no."

"Why?"

He didn't say anything for a few seconds. When I was about to repeat my question, he simply grabbed me around the waist and pulled me into him as he slammed his lips down on my mouth. I was so shocked, I didn't have time to react, and before I knew it, his tongue was invading my mouth, seeking out my tongue. I could taste the alcohol in his mouth and it was bitter and pervasive. I thrust my hands against his chest, trying to push him away, but he only held on to me tighter.

He pushed his pelvis into mine at the same time that I felt his hands suddenly moving up my thighs and underneath my skirt. Needing to free myself from him, I slammed my head back, banging it into the truck behind me accidentally. There was a momentary pain but the need to get myself out of this situation was foremost in my mind.

"Stop!" I said once my mouth was free.

"Mmm, you feel so good." He smiled down at me and his hands circled my ass while he pulled me against his obvious erection. At the thought of how hard he was, I felt sick to my stomach.

"I'm serious, Beau, let go of me."

"Stop playing hard to get, baby." He continued to grab my ass and I continued to try to separate myself from him. But because of the fact that he was much bigger than I was, I was basically at his mercy. There was no way I was forcing him away from me. The only way I was going to be able to extricate myself from him was with words.

"I'm not playing hard to get," I insisted. "I'm just not interested in having sex with you. So that means I want you to let go of me and I want you to do it now or I'm going to start screaming."

He immediately released me and stepped back, thank God. I took a deep breath and smoothed my skirt down as the sweet feeling of relief flooded me. Now I just had to get away from him and back to my room.

"What's your fucking deal?"

"I have no deal." I attempted to sidestep him before this conversation became any uglier. But he grabbed me by my upper arm and held me in place as I pulled against him, but it did no good.

"In case you don't remember, I've already fucked you," he spat at me. "So, you need to stop whatever stupid game you're playing, because I've already been between your legs, so it's not like this is the first time."

"Let go of me." I forcefully yanked my arm back. He released me at the same time, and I immediately started to wobble in my high heels. It felt like time stood still as I wondered if I could right myself, but I lost my balance and fell. I landed right on my ass on the cold cement as my purse landed beside me, everything inside spilling all over the sidewalk. I could feel my cheeks burning with humiliation as Beau looked down at me and laughed.

"You weren't worth the effort anyway," he said with a snicker as he shook his head, grabbed his keys from his pocket and started for the driver's side of his truck.

I forced myself to keep my cool as I pushed back up to my feet and, reaching for my purse, began collecting all my things. I heard the sound of Beau turning the engine on, and once he pulled into the street, I turned to watch the taillights glowing red as he turned the corner and disappeared from view.

And that was when I lost it. Tears immediately started bleeding from my eyes as I tried to catch my breath and talk myself down off the ledge. But it didn't do any good. I'd never felt so humiliated before. Actually, I felt more than just humiliation. My emotions were running the gamut from fear that Beau was going to force himself on me to regret that I'd ever even considered going out with him again, to anger that he would talk to me the way he had and finally to intense shame and humiliation based on his parting words.

At the thought that I would have to go upstairs and face Dani and tell her everything that just happened, I cried even harder. I couldn't stomach the idea of facing anyone, not when I was so mortified. Instead, I took a seat on the curb, relishing the fact that I was surrounded by darkness and no one could see me. Yes, it was cold outside, but I couldn't say I cared.

No sooner did the thought cross my mind than my phone started buzzing with an incoming call. I reached for it, wondering if it might be Beau and all the while hoping it was so I could give him a piece of my mind. But the caller ID revealed it was Derek. Why he was calling me at eleven at night I didn't know, but I also didn't want to find out. So, I didn't answer it. Instead, I watched the screen as the phone vibrated in my hand two times, then three. On the fourth vibration, I clicked to answer although I wasn't sure why.

"Hello?" I did my best to sound like I wasn't crying.

"Why'd it take you so long to answer?" He sounded perturbed.

"Um," I started before taking a deep breath as I tried to keep control of myself.

"Nik?"

"I, uh." I took another deep breath as I begged myself not to lose control. "I just was … dealing with something." I forced the words out as my voice cracked and the tears came doubly strong.

"Nikki, what's wrong? Are you okay?" He

sounded concerned, the former annoyance in his tone now completely missing.

"I don't know." I closed my eyes and tried to convince myself to stop crying. I hated the thought that I sounded completely pathetic and the last thing I wanted to do was cry in front of Derek—even if this wasn't technically in front of him. It was still bad enough.

"Where are you?"

"Sitting outside the sorority house."

"Are you alone?"

"Yeah."

"Go inside! It's not safe to be outside by yourself in the middle of the night!"

"It's not the middle of the night."

"That's not the point. You shouldn't be outside, alone in the dark."

"I don't want to see anyone."

"Well, you're going to see me because I'm on my way." I could already hear the clinking of his keys as he walked with them.

"I'm okay, Derek, you don't have to come," I started, feeling stupid that I was sitting in the dark crying by myself and now Derek was getting involved. The last thing in the world I wanted to see was the expression in his eyes when I told him what had just happened. "I don't want you to come, Derek," I said with more force this time.

"Well, get used to disappointment, because I

don't give a shit what you want. I'm on the way."

"I'm okay, really."

"And that's why you're crying by yourself outside in the dark?" I didn't respond, so he continued. "Stay where you are. I'll be there in two minutes."

He hung up the phone, probably because he didn't want me to try to argue with him. I put my phone back in my purse as I dropped my head into my hands and wished I hadn't answered it. I just didn't want Derek to be involved in such a personal and stupid situation. This whole mess was my fault because Dani was right—I never should have considered having anything to do with Beau again. Maybe all of this served me right.

How can you even think that? I yelled at myself. *This is not your fault! Beau is an asshole and you're lucky he didn't try to take further advantage of you!*

I was spared the opportunity to continue to lambaste myself because headlights in the distance arrested my attention. Seconds later, Derek pulled up in front of me and killed the engine. I swallowed hard as I tried to figure out just how much I wanted to tell him.

"Nik," he said as he walked around the Bronco and, seeing me, gathered me into his arms. I wrapped my arms around him as he held me, suddenly feeling like I was safe—like nothing and no one could ever hurt me with Derek around. I exploded into a new mess of tears, partially because I knew I couldn't think of Derek the way I was thinking about him, and that realization hurt.

"What happened?" he demanded.

Even though I hadn't wanted to, I told him everything. Well, almost everything. I left out the part about the fact that I'd planned on using Beau as my target for my femme fatale training. In fact, I left *The Femme Fatale Handbook* out completely. I figured that was a little tidbit that no one, aside from Dani and me, ever needed to know about, especially since this whole Beau-seduction-attempt would go down as my worst decision to date.

After I'd managed to spit it all out in between the sobs, I collapsed back against Derek's chest and I took a deep breath.

"It's okay," he crooned into my ear. "I've got you, Nik. It's okay."

"Thank you," I whispered as I held him and closed my eyes, feeling like I was exactly where I belonged. Being in Derek's arms felt so right, so good.

It felt like I was home.

TEN
The Femme Fatale Handbook
Chapter Twelve: The Art of Subtlety

Seduction is a game, as I have said before.

It's the art of getting what you want from someone who doesn't realize you're playing him. He gives willingly and freely, never aware of the fact that you're in control. One of the best ways to ensure you win this game is to make him think he's the one calling all the shots. It's important to remember that people, in general, hate the idea of being manipulated. If he catches on to you, he will reject you because he will hate the idea that he was making decisions he didn't want to make. The key here, then, is to make him believe that he's doing things and acting in ways that are according to his own self-interests. You have to make sure he never realizes that you're the one who's really at the wheel. The puppet never wants to be aware that there's a puppeteer.

So how do you do ensure he never finds out what you're up to? First, you have to understand the ins and outs of mastering the art of subtle persuasion. Subtle persuasion is the act of dropping hints and ideas into the minds of others in such a subtle way that they mistakenly believe these thoughts are their own. They don't realize you're the one orchestrating everything, that you're the puppet master to their puppet. Think of it like you basically duping him into believing that whatever it is you want him to do is something he wants to do.

Now, before you start thinking I'm talking about hypnotism or something like that, I'm not. You drop these subtle hints while he's awake so, no, this doesn't require a trip to the local psychic or hypnotist. What you must do is start thinking in terms of being discrete, speaking in imprecise ways, dropping hints rather than coming right out and saying what you want or what you think. You have to create your own language of veiled meaning, unclear comments and indefinable suggestions that will penetrate his mind later, when you aren't in front of him and when he's thinking back on your time together. Insinuation is something that doesn't work right away—it's something that needs to sit in the subconscious for a little while. It's something that needs to build in the back of his mind before it moves to the forefront.

The power of suggestion is much more potent than directness, and it will work on a much grander level if you allow it to. All you have to do is plant the seed and his mind will take care of the rest.

Subtlety looks like this—dropping small offhand remarks about some emotional topic, maybe something that's lacking in your life or his. Think of some unfulfilled wish or desire of his or yours. When you first make a remark about whatever it is, the subject won't be important enough to be discussed at the moment. But, later, when you're apart, it will come back to visit him, and he might even be surprised by it.

The key is to figure out what it is that's lacking in his life. Is he bored? Speak in the subtle language of adventure. Is he stressed out? Speak the language of relaxation, of calmness. Learn to speak whatever language it is that he needs to hear. And when you speak this language, bring up subtle suggestions or ideas.

The key time to make these comments is when he isn't paying attention—when he's thinking about something else or he's not aware of where the conversation is headed. Then, in a very offhand manner, you just drop a little carrot which appears to be forgotten but is later picked up on. And don't only rely on your spoken language. Use the language of your body to get your point across as well as the language of words.

Seduction is the art of mystery. Remember that most people are predictable and boring. They say exactly what they think and feel and you can figure them out in a day or two. Femme fatales are the opposite. They speak their own language of insinuation and suggestion. They speak of things that are, as of yet, unfulfilled. They are never straightforward. Remember to always think of seduction as a game. He will be in the position of guessing what all your hidden remarks, subtle suggestions and veiled hints mean.

Remember, it is always easier to catch flies with honey than it is with vinegar. And the same applies with men. Rather than hitting them over the head with your wants and needs, be subtle. You will find it will get you much further.

DEREK

I couldn't remember ever being this angry before.

After Nikki finished telling me how that asshole Beau had forced his hands underneath her skirt, even after she'd told him to stop, I wanted to go pay him a visit myself. And, yes, I'd had to swallow down my jealousy at the thought that she'd willingly given herself to such an asshole in the first place. Especially when she wouldn't give herself to me and I would never treat her in such a despicable manner ever.

"Let me walk you to your room," I said as she clung to me, shivering in the cold night air. I'd already taken my jacket off and wrapped it around her shoulders, but the poor thing was still freezing.

"No." She obstinately shook her head. "I don't want to see or talk to anyone right now."

"Well, you can't stay out here, Nik." I pointed out the obvious.

"Can I come back with you to your place?" she asked, momentarily shocking me until I realized she wasn't trying to come on to me. She just really didn't want to go back to her own room. I took a deep breath and considered her request for a second or so, just to make sure I could really act the part of the gentleman and be the friend she needed.

"Of course, you can." I started toward the Bronco and opened the passenger door for her. "I have a guest room you can stay in."

"Okay," she said with a smile, the only one I'd seen from her so far this evening. "Thank you, Derek." She sniffled as she buckled herself in and then smiled at me again. "I really appreciate you being there for me."

"I'm your friend, Nik, it's what I'm here for."

She nodded. "I just want you to know how grateful I am for you."

I didn't say anything because I suddenly felt uncomfortable. Why, I wasn't sure. I just wasn't good at this nice guy stuff. Yes, of course I valued our friendship and I cared about Nikki more than I cared for any other woman save my own mother, but there was still something that just felt wrong about this. The more I thought about it, the more I realized exactly what it was. I was taking her back to my house. That was the thought that was causing me some level of concern. Why? Because whenever I took women back to my place, it was for one express purpose.

Well, you're not going to fuck her, so get those thoughts out of your head, asshole! I said to myself and instantly felt ashamed for having even thought them in the first place. What kind of selfish prick was I that Nikki was coming to me for support and all I could think about was bending her over? God,

I was such a piece of shit.

"Derek?" she asked, pulling my attention away from my inner diatribe.

"Yeah?"

"Do you think badly of me?" Her eyes were still glassy with tears. Her mascara and eyeliner had smudged all over her eyes and upper cheeks so she looked like a raccoon. I smiled at her because she looked cute as fuck.

"Badly of you?" I repeated, clearly at a loss. "Why would I think badly of you?"

She shrugged as she dropped her attention to her hands which were clasped in her lap. "For giving Beau another chance, I guess."

"No, I don't think badly of you. But I want to kill him." And that was the truth. In fact, the more I thought about his hands on her, the more I made up my mind to pay him a visit. He needed to learn a lesson the hard way—that when a woman, and especially Nikki, tells you to stop, you stop. "And you shouldn't think badly of yourself either, by the way," I added as I eyed her pointedly. "None of this was your fault."

"I just..." She sighed and shook her head. "I just feel like I brought this on myself."

"No, you didn't. No means no, Nik. It doesn't matter if you guys dated in the past or had sex or what. No means no."

She didn't respond as I pulled up to my house

and parked just out front. "Don't even think about opening your own door," I said as I unbuckled myself and jumped down to the pavement, slamming my door shut as I hurried to open hers. Once I did, I noticed she'd taken her shoes off and was now holding them in one hand, her purse in the other.

"Come here," I said as I held my arms out and motioned for her to loop her arms around my neck.

"You're going to carry me?" She gave me a surprised laugh.

"Yeah, you don't have any shoes on and I wouldn't want you to stub your toe on the uneven sidewalk." The truth was more along the lines that I just wanted to feel her in my arms again.

She didn't respond, other than to wrap her arms around me, and then I lifted her up, kicking the door closed before I turned around and carried her up the cement stairs and down the walkway to my front door. I hadn't bothered to lock the door when I'd left because I'd been in such a hurry to get to her. I turned the knob, kicking the door open with my foot before I carried her over the threshold. And, yes, the irony there wasn't lost on me.

"So, this is my place," I said as I set her down on her feet and watched her take stock of her surroundings.

"I like it." She nodded and then smiled at me.

"It's very masculine, just like I figured it would be." With the dark leather sofas and the equally dark wood dining table, coffee table and side tables, she had a point.

"The guest room is down that hall, next to the bathroom," I said as I pointed it out. "Do you want something to sleep in?"

She nodded. "Can I borrow a T-shirt?"

"Sure." I watched her start for the hallway and couldn't help but notice that she'd certainly dressed up for Beau. She was wearing a short and flowy black skirt with a rose-colored halter top. The resulting wave of jealousy that crested over me caused me to gnash my teeth. I didn't like feeling like this one bit. It was new and it was foreign and it sucked. As soon as I pictured his hands all over her, I felt my jaw go tight.

The hallway suddenly lit up when she turned the light in the bathroom on. "Oh, my God," she said in what sounded like mortification. "My makeup!"

I couldn't help laughing. "Well, luckily for you, it all washes off." I started for my bedroom and pulled open the bottom drawer of my dresser and reached for a blue T-shirt. Then I carried it into the living room and headed for the hallway. "Are you decent?" I asked before I reached the bathroom.

"Yes," she answered as she poked her head out

of the door and smiled at me. She'd washed her face and pulled her hair back into a high ponytail. I handed her the T-shirt with a quick smile.

"You know, you don't need to wear makeup. You're beautiful enough that you don't need it."

"Well, you're nice to say that." She shook her head. "But we will have to agree to disagree."

"I mean it. I'm not just blowing smoke up your ass."

"Well, thanks." She motioned to the shirt in her hand and pulled her head back into the bathroom as she closed the door behind her.

"Let me know if you need anything else, Nik," I called out as I headed for my bedroom again. "I'm just down the hall."

"I will, and thank you!"

I walked into my bedroom and took off my T-shirt and pants, draping them over the chair back. Ordinarily I slept in the buff, but I left my boxers on just in case Nikki needed anything in the night. Then I faced my oversized, king bed and, pulling the grey and white striped duvet cover back, I was about to hop in when I heard a tentative knock on the door behind me. I turned around and found Nikki standing there, wearing my blue T-shirt, which did little to hide the swells of her nipples or her long legs. The hem of the shirt hit her at the tops of her thighs. She was nothing short of exquisite, and I felt myself swallow hard.

My dick immediately started stirring, and I couldn't really blame it, considering how fucking hot she looked standing there.

"Hi," she said.

"Hi." I sounded confused and frustrated at the same time. In fact, I couldn't continue looking at her because it was doing something to me. Looking at her made me feel depressed, disheartened, and disappointed. I didn't like it. "Did you need something?"

She dropped her eyes and took a deep breath, looking flustered. "No." Then she glanced back up at me and I could see her cheeks coloring. "I wanted to ask you if I could ... could I, um, sleep next to you, in here?" She looked completely embarrassed by what she was asking and I was so surprised, I didn't answer right away.

"Maybe it's not a," she started.

"It's okay," I interrupted as I wondered if that was a good idea. Seconds later, I realized it wasn't. In fact, it was the worst idea she'd ever come up with. I didn't know how I could possibly have her in bed with me and not try to have sex with her. Fuck, why did this have to be so hard?

"I just, um," she started. "I know this sounds dumb, but I just wanted to, uh ... to feel your arms around me." Then she immediately added. "But it's totally not a big deal if that's too weird since we're just friends. Actually, now that I said it, it does sound totally weird and I'm sorry if I just made things uncomfortable." She gave me a hurried smile and started to turn around. "I'm fine sleeping in the guest room, really I am." She took a breath and then faced me again. "I don't want you to think I'm asking too much even if... maybe I am. I'm sorry if I'm coming off in a weird way because I didn't mean to. And I really really appreciate your hospitality in letting me stay here so I'm sorry if I …"

"Stop," I said as I held up a hand and she immediately choked on whatever had been about to come out of her mouth. "Fuck, just listening to you is making me nervous."

"Oh, I'm sorry." She dropped her attention to her fidgeting hands and smiled in an embarrassed sort of way.

"And if you say you're sorry one more time, I'm going to pick you up and deposit you outside where you can sleep with the woodland creatures for the rest of the night."

She glanced up at me then and smiled as a laugh escaped her mouth. "I won't say I'm sorry again then."

"Good, because I can't fucking take it." I shook my head and chuckled. "First things first, you've got to stop acting like a virgin on prom night.

"Okay." She laughed more loudly.

"And second, yes, you can sleep next to me, silly." I actually secretly loved and hated the idea that I was going to feel her body next to mine all night, that I was going to smell her and listen to her breathe.

"Thank you," she whispered.

"Don't thank me yet." I crossed my arms against my chest.

"Why?"

"Because I have to warn you that even though we've agreed to just be friends, it's not going to be easy for me to have you half naked in my bed all night. So, if you roll over and you feel something hard and incredibly long and equally thick (she laughed at that) sticking you in the thigh or the ass, that's just what happens, so don't be offended."

She smiled up at me. "I won't be offended, Derek."

"Good. And if you feel like giving said... phallus a quick and friendly visit to your mouth, that would be okay too."

"Now you're pushing your luck," she said with a big grin.

"You can't blame a guy for trying." I backed up and held my arm out, signaling that she was okay to proceed to my bed.

"I don't blame you for trying."

"Good."

"Good," she said as she started for the bed. I

held the duvet out and watched her climb into the large bed which dwarfed her. She was careful to keep my T-shirt pulled down so I wouldn't get a glimpse of anything I shouldn't.

"Comfy?" I asked once she was under the covers. She just nodded with a wide grin as I chuckled and walked around the bed, pulling the duvet out from the other side. I never slept on this side of the bed because I had a bad shoulder and it could be painful to sleep on my left side all night. I didn't say anything to Nikki, though. Instead, I climbed in next to her. I wrapped my arm around her and ran my fingers up and down the smooth skin of her back, feeling little goose bumps crop up immediately.

"Nik?" I started.

"Yeah?" Her voice was heavy with exhaustion.

"Don't ever let any man talk to you the way Beau did again, okay?" I continued to stroke her and she nodded against my chest. "You are a prize and any man would be lucky to have you," I continued, thinking it was important that she hear and understand me. "And none of what that stupid fucker said is true. You were and you are worth it."

"Thank you, Derek," she whispered, her breath tickling my stomach. I pulled her into me even closer and then leaned down, giving her a kiss on top of her head.

"Good night, beautiful."

"Good night, Derek."

ELEVEN
NIKKI

"I think I might have freaked him out," I said to Dani as I sighed and shook my head.

We were taking a run through a neighboring residential area, and I was lagging behind her. The truth was I had no energy because I hadn't been able to eat much the last two days, my friendship with Derek weighing too much on my mind.

"Why do you think that?" Dani asked. "I don't think it's possible for you to freak Derek out. You guys are too close for that."

"I haven't heard from him in two days." I

shrugged as I shook my head. "And that's not like him at all. He texts me or calls me or sometimes both every single day."

"Well, he'll have to see you in class tomorrow, right?" Dani asked as I slowed down so I could catch my breath. I leaned against a pine tree and stretched my calf muscles because they felt like they were cramping up.

"Yeah, there's always that, I guess." I thought about our Shakespeare class tomorrow at nine a.m. This would be the first class in which I'd be Derek's T.A. and I was nervous. Mainly because I wasn't sure where I stood with him, and the last thing I wanted was to sit in awkward silence for an hour.

"And nothing happened when you spent the night at his place?" Dani asked me again, for the seventh time.

"Nothing happened!" I stretched my arms above my head. "We just cuddled all night." I took a deep breath as soon as I remembered that night. It had started off so terribly but ended better than I could ever have imagined. Or not, judging from the fact that Derek had gone MIA for the last two days.

"I don't know how you controlled yourself."

I shrugged. "I mean, of course I wanted to have sex with him! God, as soon as I saw him wearing only his boxers, I thought I was going to die. He was beyond hot, but somehow, and I'm not sure how, I controlled myself." I took a breath. "Derek and I just can't go there. You know that."

"Hmm." She wrapped a stray piece of hair around her index finger like she did when she was in deep thought.

"Hmm, what?"

"Just trying to figure out what's going on between you two."

"I think I made him uncomfortable. He seemed a little awkward in the morning, or maybe I was a little awkward or maybe we both were."

"Well, that could have been because of his raging morning wood!"

We both laughed at that, even if it was true.

Yes, I'd awoken in the morning to feeling Derek's hard-on where it was pressed into my side. He, meanwhile, had been sound asleep, but as soon as I woke up, he did too, and then I was more than sure he figured out what had woken me up.

And the fucking thing had been so huge, I'd wanted to pull his boxers down just so I could see how enormous it really was. Yes, I was soaking wet (I had been all night), and I'd had half a mind to take the huge thing down my throat until I choked on it. But I didn't. I controlled myself, and now here I was.

"So, anyway, how's Luke?" I asked, not wanting to focus on the situation with Derek because it made me antsy and worried.

"Really good." Dani shrugged as we turned around and started walking back toward the ZTS house. "I mean, we're basically friends because I'm taking things crazy super slow, but I'm happy with how it's going."

"That's great." I liked Luke, and from what Derek had told me about him, he was actually a good guy, albeit a little shy. But shy was good for Dani. Shy would balance out her wild.

When we reached the ZTS house, I was shocked to find Derek's Bronco parked out front.

"Um," I started as I faced Dani in surprise.

"Guess you're going to see him before tomorrow morning after all." She gave me a big smile as she patted me on the back and started jogging toward the house. I, meanwhile, continued up the street until I reached the Bronco, and then I knocked on the window. Seeing me, Derek immediately reached over and unlocked the door, pushing it open.

"Hi," I said as soon as he did. "Wasn't expecting to see you here."

"Hey," he answered hurriedly. "Can we talk?"

"Sure." I hopped into the passenger seat and closed the door behind me. Then I turned to face him. "I haven't heard from you in a couple of days. Is everything okay?"

"Yes." But then he shook his head, while doing his best not to look at me. "And no."

"What's going on?"

He brought his attention to the scenery in front of him and exhaled as he shook his head.

"Derek?" I asked, while my heart flip-flopped in my chest. Whatever it was that was on his mind, it couldn't be good. Otherwise, he wouldn't have been taking so long to talk to me.

He turned to face me but then seemed to think better of it and faced forward again. "I got fired."

"You got what?"

"Fired."

"From Hamilton?" I asked, just to make sure he didn't have a second job as a pizza delivery guy or something equally ridiculous.

"Yep, I was fired from Hamilton." What was strange was that he didn't seem especially upset about said firing.

"So tomorrow—"

"Tomorrow I won't be teaching class, or any other class at Hamilton from here on out." He inhaled and then smiled at me. "No classes for the rest of the summer and no classes in the fall or the spring or …"

"I get it," I interrupted him as I shook my head, still trying to grasp what he was saying. "What happened? How did you get fired?"

"So, this was the part that I really didn't want to tell you," he started with a hesitant laugh. Then he stretched his head backwards and made a grunting sort of noise that hinted at the troubled thoughts that must have been racing through his head.

"But you're going to tell me anyway." I reached over and put my hand on top of his where it rested on his thigh. He glanced down at my hand but made no motion to move it. "And I'm going to be here for you. You know that."

"I don't want you to think that any of this is your fault," he started as he turned to face me with determination. But then he seemed to lose his nerve again because he stared straight ahead. "Because it isn't."

"Okay …"

But he didn't say anything. He just sat there, facing forward, like maybe he thought the windshield was going to develop lips and start speaking for him.

"Derek?"

"Right." He cleared his throat and then took another big breath. "So … I … well, ahem," he cleared his throat again.

"For the fucking love of fucking God, will you spit it out!"

He looked at me and shook his head. "You really aren't going to like this."

"Derek."

He nodded. "I went to pay a visit to Beau a couple of days ago," he began as I immediately shook my head and my stomach dropped down to my toes.

"You did what?" I was stunned. "Derek, why would you do that?!"

"Because I was pissed off that he touched you against your will, and he had no business talking to you the way he did. That's why!" He turned to face me, his eyes blazing. "And I wasn't about to let him get away with it."

That was when I noticed the side of his face. "Your eye!" I gripped his chin and forced him to face me fully. His left eye was bruised and swollen. "He hit you!" My mouth fell open in shock as anger filled me.

"Not before I got off a few of my own," he answered with a boyish laugh. "You think I look bad, you should see the other guy!" He did his best Mafioso accent.

"So, the dean found out that you hit a student and he fired you," I said, piecing together the rest of the puzzle.

"Yep." Derek sighed as he shook his head and then looked ticked off. "And understandably so, I guess."

"So, what are you going to do now?" I was worried that he'd move away and I might never see him again, even though I really had no reason to think that.

He shrugged. "Going to look for another job,

obviously, Nik." He gave me a laugh and a shrug like that much should have been obvious.

"Where?"

"Wherever they'll take me."

I faced forward as the weight of this news sunk into me. I was quiet for a few seconds as I realized I was the reason Derek had lost his job. "This is all my fault."

"No, it isn't!" He reached over and grabbed my hand, squeezing it tightly. "This is exactly why I didn't want to tell you what happened. This isn't your fault! It was my idea to go talk to the asshole, and his idea to try to take a swing at me."

"He swung at you first?"

"Yeah," he answered with a nod. "I didn't want to fight. I just wanted to have words with him."

"Did you tell the dean that he came after you first?" I didn't understand how it was that Derek had been the one to get fired if he'd told the dean exactly what had happened—that Beau had thrown the first punch.

"Yeah, but it didn't matter. The dean has been gunning for me all year and this was the perfect excuse to fire me, so he took it."

"Well, that hardly seems fair."

"It hardly is fair," he answered with that boyish grin again. "But it is what it is."

"So, what happened to Beau?" Clearly, there were still details to this story I didn't know. "Did he get kicked out or suspended, at least?"

"No, nothing happened to him," Derek answered with a sigh.

"That's bullshit!"

"You're telling me!" Then he laughed. "Funny how all I wanted to do was teach the piece of shit a lesson without any violence, and now I'm the one without a job."

"I'm sorry to hear that." Then something else occurred to me. "Did the police get involved?"

"No, thank God."

"How did the dean find out then?"

"Beau, the big baby, went to tell the dean the next day. I figure he knew he could get me fired so he played his Ace." Then he shrugged like it wasn't such a big deal. "It's okay, I wasn't happy at Hamilton anyway."

"You aren't just saying that?"

"No." Then he smiled at me. "Maybe this is fate telling me to get off my lazy ass and find another job somewhere I'd be happier."

"Maybe." I couldn't help but hope that somewhere wouldn't be far away. "So, what did you say to Beau?" I didn't want to even think about Derek moving away. He'd quickly become one of my closest friends and someone I really cared about deeply.

He shrugged. "That if he ever so much as looked at you again, he was going to deal with me."

"Really?" I was shocked and completely amazed that Derek would have gone to such extreme lengths for me. And I was totally and completely thrilled to hear it, to know he cared about me—maybe as much as I cared about him.

"Yeah, and I meant every word of it," he continued. "Then the stupid asshole decided to try to take a punch at me, but the dumbass didn't realize that my dad's a cop so I've known how to fight since I was twelve."

I frowned at him. "So how did *you* end up with a black eye then?"

"Let's just say it took one of his buddies to hold me back while Beau, the chicken shit, took a cheap shot."

"Oh my God, Derek! There were two of them and one of you!" My mouth dropped open again. "Are you hurt anywhere else? What else did they do to you?"

He shrugged. "They got my ribs pretty good." It was then that I realized he was slouching pretty obviously in his seat.

"Oh my God," I said for the nth time. "Are they broken? Have you been to the hospital to get checked out?"

"No, no hospital."

"Derek."

"I'm fine, Nikki."

"How do you know?"

"Because my ribs aren't broken, but they're bruised pretty good." Then he faced me with another boyish grin. "But I fared better than they did."

"So that's why I haven't heard from you for the last two days." I crossed my arms against my chest and regarded him coolly. "Which I'm not happy about, by the way. You should have told me what happened so I could have taken care of you."

"I'm a manly man, Nik. I didn't want some woman doting over me," he finished with a laugh.

"Oh, some woman, huh?" I gave him a look as he laughed and shrugged like he was innocent of any wrongdoing. "Well, I'm glad to know you're okay, although I wish you had told me all of this earlier. I was worried about you and … us."

"Worried about us?"

"Well, yeah, I usually hear from you every day, so not hearing anything from you for two days is weird. You should have returned my texts, you asshole," I finished as I playfully swatted him in the arm.

"Yeah." He dropped his attention to the steering wheel and seemed pensive again.

"Okay, what else is going on? I know that look of yours."

"I guess you do know me too well." He looked over at me and smiled almost sadly. "I've been keeping to myself the last couple of days because I needed time and space to think. It wasn't just about the fight with Beau or the fact that I got fired."

"To think? About what?"

"About you," he answered honestly as he faced me again and his eyes seemed heavy, weighted somehow.

"What about me?" My heart began pounding and I wondered if he was going to tell me we'd made a mistake sleeping next to each other and now we couldn't continue to be friends because he knew I'd fallen for him and he didn't feel the same way.

He was quiet for another few seconds, but then he turned to face me and opened his mouth but no words came out.

"What, Derek?" I prompted him, hating the idea that he was going to keep me in limbo for another second. No matter how bad the news was, I'd rather have it out in the open than go through another moment feeling like this. "Spit it out. I'm strong; I can take it."

"I'm in love with you, Nikki."

TWELVE
The Femme Fatale Handbook
Chapter Thirteen: How to Play the Sex Game

Okay, so you're now ready to take your relationship with your guy to the next level?

He's given you some level of commitment and you like him enough or want something from him badly enough that you're willing to let him sample your pot of honey. Reminder—if you haven't read the section about when it's the right time for sex, go back and read it!

For the rest of you, let's delve right in.

In this section, I'm going to tell you how to get a guy into your bedroom. Yes, you could just ask and he'll most likely say yes, but you're a seductress, so you don't go the direct route! But all of this information is stuff you need to know!

1. Find out what turns him on! The best way to find out what a guy is into is to ask. But do so in a non-direct, flirty and playful sort of way. Maybe make a game out of it. Find out what sort of lingerie he likes, what positions are his favorite, whether he likes romantic sex or naughty sex. The list goes on! But once you have this information, you can use it to your advantage!

2. Remember to use your voice to aid your cause! A soft, sensual, feminine voice is a huge turn on to men. Think about how popular phone sex lines used to be. All it took was a woman with a sexy voice saying naughty things. Remember that practice makes perfect, so try subtly making your tone of voice softer and more sensual. And, yes, when it comes to sex, men really like it when you moan, talk and otherwise make sounds!

3. Send him flirty text messages and send him sexy photos. It didn't take a genius to come up with this one. If you send a man a sexual text message, he's going to like it and you're going to have a captive audience. Furthermore, men like naked photos. They are just men, after all, and they are visual creatures. Remember that if you decide to send a man an explicit image, make sure you trust him to be the type to keep it to himself! A note about dirty talk: If you can do it. Do. The end.

4. Take a clue from Cleo: Remember how you learned that Cleopatra was expertly good at becoming all women? She was theatrical and constantly changing up her makeup, hair and wardrobe. Men like variety and they can get easily bored, so borrow Cleo's trick and make it work for yourself. Think librarian one day, schoolgirl the next, goddess the next. Not only is it a fun way to keep him guessing, but it's fun to play dress up too!

5. Sexual Innuendo: The best way to get your physical seduction going is to phrase your statements in a way that is full of sexual innuendo aka say things that might not necessarily be dirty in a dirty way. Men love anything that hints at the sexual, and this is one way to really rev up his sexual engine!

6. Make him jealous! Remember when I talked about the power of being popular? Well, it's true sexually as well. Don't be afraid to flirt with other men in front of him. Nothing too extreme—don't start making out with some random guy—but it's perfectly fine to be friendly and flirty with guys in front of him. It will stoke his jealousy and he'll be even more inclined to want to claim you.

7. Don't be afraid to show you're turned on!

This might seem like an obvious one, but allow me to explain. When you are turned on by a guy, nature takes care of the rest. Your lips plump, you get a flush to your cheeks, you release pheromones ... all of these contribute to subliminally communicate the fact that you are sexually turned on to your partner. In order to trigger the sexual goddess within, you'll want to embrace your own desire. Allow yourself to be aroused while you talk to him, and you'll find your sexual stimulation will echo in your body language and the way you look.

8. And finally, get naked! Lose the clothes and he'll definitely rise to the occasion, literally and figuratively. And, yes, I get that this is probably a pretty obvious point too, but there is getting naked for a guy and then there's the seductress's way of getting naked for a guy. The best way to do this in my opinion? Casually get completely naked and intentionally allow your guy to see you on full display while simultaneously acting completely unconcerned that he's totally turned on. Combining nudity, unabashed confidence and nonchalant sexual desire... That's the way of the femme fatale.

###
DEREK

Now that the words were out, I felt some level

of relief.

But then Nikki wasn't responding, and any relief I'd experienced quickly went packing as I wondered if I'd just made a huge mistake.

"Um, what?" she said finally as she faced me and appeared to be in total shock.

"Um, I love you." I chuckled because this conversation wasn't exactly going the way I'd hoped it would. Yes, it was true—I was in love with her. And it's not like this was a realization that had just sprung up on me either. The truth was that I'd been in love with her for weeks, but I'd also been so pigheaded that I'd refused to admit it to myself.

But once the situation between Nikki and Beau had happened and the resulting anger I'd experienced, I'd known the truth. There was no way I would have been as furious if I hadn't been in love with Nikki. Furthermore, I never would have, not in a million years, gotten into a physical confrontation with some chump over a woman. But I could honestly say that I would have relived the whole thing over again for Nikki. A dozen times over. She meant that much to me.

"Derek, you screwed this whole thing up," she said finally, frowning at me while she crossed her arms against her chest.

"Um, what?"

She smiled even more broadly. "You weren't

supposed to tell me you love me *like that!*"

"I wasn't aware there was a protocol for telling a woman you're in love with her." I was completely taken aback by her reaction. If nothing else, I could always count on Nikki's unpredictability.

"Of course, there is!" She threw her hands into the air like I was the dumbest man she'd ever met. And who the hell knew—maybe I was, but this love stuff was totally new to me.

"Explain."

She frowned at me. "You don't tell me in the middle of the day after you also just told me you got fired, while sitting in your Bronco and dressed like that!" She looked at my sweatshirt and jeans with disgust. "Meanwhile, I'm sweaty and gross and still in my running clothes!" She shook her head. "What's wrong with you?!"

"I'm sorry?" I gave her a shrug as I tried to understand just what exactly was going on here. I couldn't tell if she was happy to know I was in love with her or … not.

"I'm going to allow you a do-over," she informed me with a clipped nod. "Tonight you can take me out to dinner at a nice restaurant that we both will dress up for and you can tell me then."

"Oh, is that so?" I fought to keep from grabbing her and pulling her into me and kissing her to show her just how much she meant to me.

But, apparently, there was a natural progression to these sorts of things, and I didn't think an impromptu kiss attack would fit the bill.

"Yes, that's so."

"Well, what if I decide I'd rather just take it back?"

Her eyes went wide. "You can't take it back!"

I laughed and held my hands up in a faux rendition of surrendering. "Okay, okay, sheesh, don't attack the guy with the black eye." I shook my head and then we both just looked at each other for a few seconds as we stopped laughing. "And as for tonight—it's a date. I'll pick you up at seven."

"Very good." She jumped down from the Bronco, then turned to face me as she rested her hand on the door. "Seven it is." Then she grinned from ear to ear as she shut the door and I started the engine, wondering just what in the hell went through that girl's head. Whatever it was though, I was hooked.

###

"Okay, so when do I say it again?" I asked once we were comfortably seated across from one another.

I'd chosen a French restaurant that I'd heard was good and one I'd been wanting to try. I was dressed in black slacks and a white, collared shirt which Nikki had, thankfully, approved of. As far as her attire went, I approved and then some, because she was wearing a tight, black cocktail dress with a cute red sweater and high black heels. She'd left her hair down and it flowed around her shoulders, just how I liked it best.

"You can say it now," she said as she took a sip of her wine and faced me expectantly.

"Okay, here goes."

"Minus the 'here goes'."

I cleared my throat and gave her a look as I tried not to laugh. "I, Derek Anderson, would like to profess my undying love for you, Nicole Sloan." I faced her expectantly. "How was that?"

She nodded. "That was very good."

"And, do you have anything to say?" I downed my glass of wine and motioned to the waiter for another. Luckily, he spotted me from across the room so he didn't interrupt us.

"Why do I need to say anything?" She did her best to attempt to conceal her smile.

"Oh, I don't know, maybe because it would be nice to let me know how you feel about me?"

"Oh, hmm." She pretended to ponder the question, even going so far as to look up at the ceiling as she bobbed her fingers against her chin like she was deep in thought. Then she smiled widely. "I, Nicole Sloan, am completely and have been completely in love with you, Derek Anderson, from the moment I met you."

"Hmm," I grumbled as I sighed audibly.

"What?"

"Yours sounded better than mine."

She laughed as she shook her head and took another sip of her Riesling. "So, what happens now?"

I shrugged. "I guess this is the part where I ask you to be my girlfriend and I take you off the market?"

She giggled and I was suddenly consumed with happiness just to see how happy she was. And that was a weird thing for me—something I'd never experienced before, but I could honestly say I liked the way it felt. A lot.

"So this is a pretty big step for the quintessential bachelor?" she asked, bringing up a subject I knew she would. And it was just as well because it was something that needed to be discussed.

"The quintessential bachelor believes it's time he grew up," I answered honestly. She looked surprised. "I know what you are, Nik, and you're a prize—just like I said the other night. And I'm a smart enough man to know when I've stumbled across something that could just be the best thing that's ever happened to me."

"I'm sure you understand my concerns though?" She chewed on her lower lip like she did when she was being contemplative.

"Of course." I nodded. "But I want to assure you that I know how I feel about you. It's not like this is a short-lived crush that's going to go away. I know you, Nik. We've been friends for a while now, and my feelings for you have never changed."

"Maybe that's just because we've never had sex?" she countered. "I don't mean to play devil's advocate, but I also want to look out for myself and for our friendship too. I would never want a relationship that doesn't work out to ruin what we have now, Derek." She paused as she glanced down at her wine. "Your friendship means the world to me."

"I get that because I feel the same way about you and us. I love our friendship, you must know that?" I did get it—this was a risk and there was a lot at stake. It made sense. Of course, it did, but that didn't mean I was going to give up on what could be more between us. "But I'm asking you to trust me."

"To trust you?"

I nodded. "If you care about me the same way I care about you, please give me the benefit of the doubt."

"And if you change your mind?"

"I won't," I answered immediately, nearly cutting her off.

"What happens if we have sex and you lose

interest in me?"

"It won't happen." My expression was sincere.

"Just pretend for a second that it does, what then?"

I took a deep breath and stalled. I didn't want to answer her question because I was convinced sex would only make our connection stronger and I was dying to experience her. I had been all along. No, sex between us would be explosive. I knew that. "I will never let anything get in the way of what we have now, Nik. If it doesn't work out between us, I'm telling you now that I would do everything in my power to preserve our friendship."

She was quiet for a few seconds as she continued to gnaw her lower lip. Then she nodded. "I believe you, and I would do the same."

"But let me make something very clear to you," I continued as she glanced up at me, curiosity in her eyes. "I know that I'm in love with you. I've never been in love with someone before, so however I felt about women in my past isn't something you can use to try and figure out how I will be with you. It's like comparing apples to oranges, because I never felt for anyone the way I feel for you."

"Okay." She still sounded reluctant to fully believe me.

"Just trust me, Nik, please." I reached across

the table and took her hand. "Can you do that?"

"Yes," she answered with a quick nod.

"Thank fucking God." I gave her a small laugh. "So, next question, when the hell can I take you off the market?"

She didn't pull her eyes from mine. "I've been off the market for a while, Derek, you just never knew it."

THIRTEEN
NIKKI

So, yes, I let Derek take me off the market.

Really, what other choice did I have? Yes, I was scared that sex between us could end up ruining our friendship as well as this budding romantic relationship we were now in, but I figured I had to take a chance. Because it was simple—I was in love with Derek and I wanted to be with him. I wanted us to work. So, I had to trust him by giving him the benefit of the doubt.

And, yes, I was fully aware that throughout our

conversation, I hadn't exactly been wearing my femme fatale hat. Maybe that was a mistake, I wasn't sure. All I knew was that I needed to be straight with Derek because our friendship meant the world to me and he needed to understand that if we took this huge step, we might never be able to come back from it.

When we were finished with dinner, I felt my anxiety begin to double, which felt strangely like a bunch of insects humming in my stomach. Of course, I was excited, thrilled and beyond enthusiastic at the prospect of seeing Derek naked and then feeling him inside me, but I was also worried. Worried about what would happen in the morning.

Nothing is going to happen in the morning! I told myself. *Because you are going to remember your femme fatale training and you're going to use it! That's what got you to this point with Derek anyway. You stood out in a way women before you haven't, and because of that, you were able to snag him where so many others failed. So, buck up and remember that Derek is right—you are a prize, so start acting like one!*

But I wasn't all right. Sure, the femme fatale training had helped me to keep my head held high and to learn how to have the utmost confidence but it wasn't what had made Derek love me. Derek had fallen for me for me—not because of some game

I'd played on him. He loved me for me. Where the femme fatale stuff had helped me was in realizing I was a prize and Derek was lucky to have me. Likewise, though, he was a prize and I was lucky to have him. The thing that I had to keep in mind was my own sense of self-love and confidence. If I did that, there was no room for fear.

After Derek paid the bill, we walked out of the restaurant toward the Bronco, hand in hand. I was happy—I couldn't deny it. I was happier than I'd been in a long time because I felt like I was exactly where I belonged. Derek was right for me in so many ways, and it was so wonderful to realize that he, too, had finally reached that same conclusion.

"So, where are you thinking of looking for a job?" I asked as he unlocked my door and opened it for me, leaning in to give me a peck on my lips as I buckled myself in.

"Let's talk about it." He closed my door and reemerged on the other side, then he settled himself into his seat, turned on the engine and reached over, squeezing my lower thigh as he smiled at me and I felt my cheeks color. I just wasn't used to this type of affection from him and it felt different. Amazing, yes, but different also. It was going to take some getting used to.

"Okay," I said. "Did you have any colleges in mind?"

"Well, as you know, there really isn't anything

in this area other than Hamilton." He looked over at me with a shrug. "So, I was thinking of looking at any universities within an hour's drive."

"Hmm." I thought about it and, in doing so, it started to worry me.

"I'm not about to move away from you now that we've started a relationship, Nik." He laughed. "So, if that's what you're worried about, stop."

"I'm not." I took a deep breath. "I'm just …"

"Worrying about it," he finished for me with that boyish laugh of his that drove me crazy. "Let's not think about it now." He patted my knee consolingly. "I just want to talk about you and you and me."

I smiled at him and then glanced outside my window, recognizing Magnolia Street as he took a left on it. From what I could tell, it appeared he was driving me back to the ZTS house. "Where are we going?" I asked with a frown.

"I'm dropping you back off?" Now he was the one who sounded surprised.

"Why?"

He cleared his throat. "I don't want you to rush into anything you aren't ready for yet, Nikki," he started. "And I want to prove to you that I'm serious about this relationship. I figured a good way to do that is to show you that I can wait until you're ready for us to get intimate with each other."

"Okay..." I frowned and I could feel it all the way to my feet. A frown that hinted at my total and complete disappointment. "I get that and I appreciate it, Derek, but I want you to take me back to your place right now."

"Are you sure?" He gave me a pointed expression.

"Yes, of course, I'm sure." There was no way I was going to let him drive away without us hooking up. I mean, come on—we'd both been chomping at the bit for this.

He nodded. "We can go back to my place but that doesn't mean we have to have sex, Nik. We can sleep next to each other again like we did a few nights ago."

"When the hell did you turn into such a prude?" I batted his arm playfully.

He laughed. "We both know I'm not," he started and then paused as he took a deep breath and nodded at me. "But I want you to know that I'm happy just to be with you. I don't need more than that. I'm trying to do this... the right way, Nikki. And maybe I'm screwing up."

"Stop." I reached over and put my index finger over his lips to shush him. "I've wanted to have sex with you for so long now that there's no way I'm going to let you tell me no on the exact night we should be doing it!"

He chuckled and shook his head as he stole a

glance at me. "I don't know how I got so lucky."

"You must have done something good in a past life," I responded with a laugh as he squeezed my thigh again.

###

I was nervous, there was no denying it.

As I stood in Derek's bedroom, waiting for him to come out of the restroom, I couldn't help the butterflies in my stomach.

What is wrong with you? I asked myself. *It's not like you've never had sex before! Stop freaking out!*

Of course, I'd had sex before, but I'd never had sex with Derek, and that thought was making me so uptight, I felt like I might throw up. I paced back from one side of the room to the other and then back again as I chewed my lower lip and tried to talk myself down. Yes, I knew there was nothing to be afraid of and I was working myself up for nothing, but I couldn't seem to stop.

When Derek came out of the bathroom, I noticed he'd taken his shirt off and it was all I could do to keep myself from staring at the tan, muscled chest and arms before me. There was a sprinkling of dark hair around his nipples and a little trail that started beneath his belly button and disappeared into the hemline of his jeans. He was nothing short of magnificent.

"You okay, Nik?" he asked with a chuckle as he walked over and looped his arms around me, pulling me into him. "You look nervous."

"I'm okay." I didn't want him to know how edgy I really was.

"I'm not going to bite." He glanced down at me and smiled. "Unless you want me to."

"Ha ha," I answered as I inhaled a deep breath and then wrapped my arms around him again, wanting to feel his warmth against my skin. I continued to breathe in deeply as I attempted to calm my heart and talk myself out of feeling so damned nervous.

"We don't have to do this, Nik, if you aren't ready." He gave me that devil's smile again and suddenly I wanted him inside me now.

"Too much talking." He chuckled but I cut his laugh short. "Kiss me," I whispered as he brought his hands to either side of my face and then closed the gap between us, bringing his lips to mine. I pushed myself into him and opened my lips so I could feel and taste him. His tongue immediately entered my mouth and mated with mine and I closed my eyes in response.

"Say it," he said suddenly as he pulled away from me.

I glanced up at him in surprise because I wasn't sure what he was asking me at first. But after I witnessed the passion in his eyes, I knew what he wanted from me. "I love you."

"Say it again," he ordered as he dropped down to his knees and brought either of his hands to the hemline of my dress. He pushed it up my thighs, all the way to my navel as his eyes hungrily roamed over my stomach and my black lace panties. I immediately felt myself gushing, the stinging sensation between my legs throbbing.

"I love you."

Remember every second of this, Nikki, I told myself. *Because you'll never have this exact moment again. Cherish it.*

"Again," Derek said as he brought his finger to my lace panties and gently teased my clit through the lace. I immediately threw my head back and moaned. "Nikki," he said gruffly, pulling my attention back to him. I looked down at him and ran my fingers down the side of his face as he looked at me.

"I love you," I managed, as seconds later, he pushed my panties to the side and then his mouth was on me, licking and sucking my clit as I gripped his hair and held his head in place, gyrating my hips against him.

"God, you taste so fucking good," he said as he broke the seal between us and looked up at me, his eyes radiating his need. He took his index finger and, starting at my clit, walked it down all the way to my entrance. Still watching me, he circled my opening with his finger, pulling away as soon as I tried to push down on it.

"Mmm, you'll get my finger when I say you will." He looked up at me and I watched him. Then he brought his mouth back to my clit, but rather than licking me, he inhaled deeply. "And I love the way you smell. Just the smell of you is making me rock hard."

He brought his index finger to my opening again and pushed his finger inside me as I bucked above him, moaning while I gripped his hair more tightly. I rocked against him, loving the feel of his finger as he pushed it in and out of me.

"Take off your dress," he ordered as he pulled his finger out of me and backed away a few steps so he could watch me.

"Please don't stop."

"Be a good girl and take off your dress for me and I'll give you what you want."

I didn't argue. Instead, I pulled my dress up and over my head. Derek's eyes fastened on my black bra.

"Take it off." I was thrilled to my core because I hadn't imagined he'd be this confident and dominant in the bedroom. But then I thought about who he was and his dominance suddenly made total sense. In fact, I couldn't imagine him being any other way.

I unclasped my bra and pulled it down one arm and then the other, going as painstakingly slowly as I could. When my breasts were bare, I noticed him staring at them with unabashed desire.

"You are even more beautiful than I imagined," he said, his tone gruff. "And I need you back in my mouth." I didn't waste any more time and immediately took the steps that separated us as he gripped me by the hips. He started sucking on my clit again as I rocked against his face, loving the way he was making me feel. He pushed his index finger back inside me as I bucked against him.

I was currently in the throes of an orgasm and, as if sensing my upcoming release, he suddenly pulled his finger out of me and smiled lasciviously.

"Please, Derek," I groaned.

"Not yet." Then he lifted me bride style and carried me to his bed, gently laying me down on my back. He pushed my legs apart and brought his tongue back to my wetness as I writhed underneath him, the pleasure so intense it almost bordered on agony.

"Please," I whispered again as I gripped his hair and held him in place. "Please, Derek."

"What do you want, my love?" He pulled his face up and smiled at me as if he knew exactly what I wanted.

"You," I answered on a moan.

He didn't say anything but stood up and started removing his jeans. I sat up so I could watch him. He pulled his boxers and his jeans down his long legs, and when his erection sprang forward, I found I was transfixed by it.

"Oh, my God, you're huge!" I said, sounding both worried and awed.

"I'm glad you approve," he chuckled. I, meanwhile, couldn't take my eyes off him. He was perfect and it was true—he *was* perfectly huge. I was definitely a little bit nervous to take him inside me, but as soon as he crawled on top of me and pushed me down against the bed and kissed me, the fear subsided. He held himself at my opening and then pushed himself forward, his tip entering me as I moaned underneath him, my mouth still playing captive to his. He rocked his hips forward and pushed more of himself into me as I arched against him and, wrapping my arms around him, gripped his back with my nails. He was easily the largest guy I'd ever been with.

"Mmm, you're so tight, Nikki," he whispered in my ear as he broke the seal of our lips.

He pushed into me a tiny bit farther as my eyes widened and another moan escaped me. He was definitely big, and I could feel myself stretching to accommodate him. I wrapped my legs around him and hoisted myself up, wanting to bury the rest of him in me. He held my gaze but didn't make any motion to give me more. And then, in one motion, he gripped my ass, pulling me up off the bed at the same time that he thrust the whole thing all the way into me as I slammed my nails into his back and screamed.

"God, you feel so good," I sang at him as he pushed inside me harder, hurrying his pace with each thrust.

"Look at me, Nik," he ground out as soon as I closed my eyes. I opened them again and held his gaze as he continued to push himself in and out of me, both of us moaning and staring at each other in a way I'd never experienced before. Truly, before this, I'd never understood what sex was—what it could feel like. Actually, scratch that, I'd never understood what making love was. But now I did.

"I love you," he whispered as I tightened my hold around him and heard my moaning scream as my body erupted in a shuddering orgasm.

DEREK

Nikki was pure heaven.

She tasted so sweet, and as I watched her taking all of me, it was all I could do not to explode right there. But I didn't because I wanted to make this last.

Instead, I pushed inside her harder, pushing

with everything I had so I could watch her heavy breasts bounce up and down. When I couldn't taste her on my mouth or lips anymore, I pulled myself out of her and then slammed her legs apart as I buried my face into her, needing to taste her ambrosia, needing to fill my mouth with her juice.

And then it wasn't enough for me that I tasted her, I wanted her to taste her own sweetness, so I reached down and gripped her around the waist as I flipped her onto her hands and knees. I was facing her ass so I smacked it, loving the way her flesh jiggled beneath my hand.

"Turn around, I want your mouth on me," I ordered. She did as she was told and smiled up at me as I stuck my thumb into her mouth and pulled down, making sure she opened her mouth wide. Then I slid in past those pink lips and farther still until her entire mouth enveloped me.

I continued to push into her mouth, until I could feel the back of her throat and she started to gag on me, then I pulled back. Her eyes watered as she looked up at me. She began moaning as she reached down and started rubbing her clit and I had to stop myself from creaming into her mouth.

"Now turn around."

"Mmm, yes, sir," she said as she turned around and lifted her ass into the air, bending the rest of her body down so that it touched the bed. She spread her legs as I gripped either of her cheeks.

"I like it when you call me 'sir'," I admitted, never having had a woman refer to me as such and I had to admit, I did like it.

"Not as much as I like taking the whole length of you," she managed and in response, that's exactly what I gave her. Until I could feel the end of her. She was so tight and slick, it was all I could do to hold myself back. I pulled out and then shoved myself all the way back in again as she screamed underneath me, and when her inner walls started to seize around me, I realized she was having an orgasm. And at that realization, I couldn't hold mine back any longer. When I pulled out of her, I allowed myself to release all over her ass.

"Oh, my God," I said as I felt like I was going to pass out.

"I second that," she said as she smiled up at me.

I could barely move. "Come here," I whispered to her as I collected her in my arms and pulled her into my chest and we both lay on my bed, panting.

And, if it was even possible, I was even more in love with her now.

FOURTEEN
The Femme Fatale Handbook
Chapter Fourteen: How to Make the Spell Last

So, you've successfully landed your target, what happens now?

Maybe you now find yourself in a relationship or maybe you've gotten whatever it was that you wanted from this guy and you're over it? Well, first things first, congratulations! You've done well.

Now I know you're probably wondering how to keep your happily ever after? Good thing you asked, because this is an important question.

Now that you've snared the object of your affections, your seduction doesn't suddenly stop. You must continue to do all the things you were doing in order to win his affections the first time around. Just because you find yourself in a relationship, etcetera, doesn't mean it's time to stop caring. On the contrary! If you want to keep him, you have to school him on how not to take you for granted and you have to school yourself on how to make sure he doesn't grow bored with you. And if you grow bored with him? It's time to move on to your next conquest!

If you've decided you got whatever it was you wanted from him and you're ready to part ways, you're in an easier boat. Simply cut all your ties and do it quickly. The longer you both hang on, the uglier the situation will get. If, on the other hand, you want to keep him, read on!

1. Fight against the natural urge to stop trying. If you've been acting a certain way with him up until now and you stop trying as hard, he will think you're manipulative and that you only acted the way you did to get what you wanted. This could definitely backfire, so resist the urge to relax! The best way to ensure this doesn't happen is to continue doing what you were doing—continue to make him feel special, all the while keeping him on the edge of his seat by maintaining your mystery and intrigue. Even though he might have captured you in a relationship, that doesn't mean he owns or controls you. You are still an independent, femme fatale who answers to no one, save yourself!

2. Don't forget to keep the mystery! There's a famous quote that says "familiarity breeds contempt," which is the idea that once someone knows you intimately well, they view you in a negative light. I believe this to be true, and I also believe it's spurred by boredom. As an example, I want you to consider video games. They usually appeal to men, right? I've seen boyfriends spend hour upon hour, day after day, trying to beat a certain game. They become obsessed with it. And guess what happens once they conquer the game? They never play it again. Don't become the beaten game! Continue to shroud yourself in mystery, otherwise the familiarity between you both will lead to dullness. Just how do you maintain the mystery? Continue to keep him guessing, don't suffocate him by constantly being available—absence really does make the heart grow fonder because it allows you both space to miss each other. Don't ever let him think he has you figured out. That will signify the beginning of the end.

3. Resist the urge to take things more seriously now that you're in a relationship. Remember how you won him over in the first place! It was through a fun, charismatic, mysterious and playful persona. Just because you're now in a relationship with him, that fun side of your personality shouldn't disappear! Instead, encourage those parts of your personality that he fell in love with and you'll find you stay a happier person when you're focused on spreading happiness. Never become the nagging girlfriend—that will put the final nail in the coffin.

Most of all, remember the road you took in order to reach your final destination. It is a road that you can travel more than once—back and forth repeatedly. After all, you are a seductress, a femme fatale, which means you hold the cards—all the power and the control. You make your own destiny and it is up to you who you bring along with you for the ride.

###

NIKKI
TWO WEEKS LATER

"What about this?" I asked Dani as I held up my pink bikini.

"Yeah, that's good, bring that."

I threw the bikini into my open suitcase and turned back to raiding my closet. Yes, I was packing my bags for a trip. A trip that just happened to see me traveling to Thailand with the man who had started as the target of my seduction, but turned into the man of my dreams and my best friend, well save for Dani, of course.

"Dude, you better hurry, they're going to be here soon," Dani said from where she was lying on her bed, highlighting the sections of *The Femme Fatale Handbook* that she wanted to revisit later. She was taking this seductress stuff pretty seriously. Her bags were already packed and waiting for her patiently beside her bed.

I glanced up at the clock and swore because I still hadn't packed my toiletries. "Ugh, I've gotta hurry and I still haven't even looked through my box of makeup and bathroom shit."

Dani sat up and put the notebook in the drawer in her bedside table as she headed for my side of the room. She reached down underneath my bed and pulled out the box in which I kept my bathroom items.

"I'm going to pack up all your toiletries so you concentrate on your clothes," she said as she smiled up at me. "And good job waiting so long to do this, by the way."

"Yeah, yeah."

"You'd think you could have taken, oh, I don't know, maybe twenty minutes away from Derek so you could have started packing earlier? I swear you two are like rabbits!"

She was right. Derek and I *were* like rabbits.

I'd never had so much sex before in my life, but I wasn't complaining! I glanced down at her and laughed. "Yeah, we're pretty gross, aren't we?"

"No, you're cute." She waved me away with an unconcerned hand. "And to think you were so freaked out that he was going to lose interest in you!"

I sighed as I remembered the panic I'd experienced the morning after we'd had sex. I'd been completely freaked out for no reason at all because Derek was even more attentive and loving now, two weeks later. Our relationship had deepened into the most incredible sexual and loving friendship that I could have ever hoped for.

I didn't get a chance to respond to Dani because I was interrupted by a quick knock on our door. Dani stood up, dropping my bag full of toiletries into my suitcase, and then opened the door, revealing Derek standing in the hallway. Luke was right beside him. Derek smiled at Dani, giving her a hug as he walked into our room and his attention shifted to my opened suitcase where it sat on the bed.

"You still aren't finished packing?" he faux yelled, throwing his hands up in the air. "Nik, we've gotta be at the airport in an hour!"

"I know, I know." I threw the pile of clothes beside the suitcase into it and then struggled with the zipper. Derek shook his head and walked over to me, giving me a kiss before he pushed me aside and zipped the thing up himself.

"Hi, Nik," Luke said as he walked into the room and Dani shut the door behind him. I walked over to him and hugged him as Dani handed me my carry-on. Luke, meanwhile, walked across the room and gripped each of her bags.

"We are all packed up and ready to go!" Dani nearly sang. "Thailand, here we come!"

"I'm so excited!" I said as I turned to face Derek, who was already holding my suitcase and starting for the door. "I have a bunch of brochures for us to look through on the plane so we can decide what we want to do once we get there, and I went ahead and made an outline of all the things I think look the most interesting. Just to make it easier on everyone," I added with a smile as the four of us emptied into the hallway.

"She's a planner," Dani explained to Luke with a shrug as I turned around, remembering to lock our door. When I turned back again, I found all three of them facing me, and I suddenly found myself beaming from ear to ear.

"This is going to be a trip we will never forget, I can just feel it," I said with a rush of excitement.

And I really meant it.

The End

Stay tuned for more sexy contemporary romances coming soon!

Be sure to join my email list at www.hpmallory.com so you'll be the first to know when part two becomes available!

Looking for something else to read while you wait for the second part of Age Gap Romance?

Try my Bestselling Lily Harper series!

Read on for chapter one of Better Off Dead, the first book in this bestselling series!

BETTER OFF DEAD
Lily Harper #1
by H.P. Mallory

"Midway upon the journey of our life, I found myself within a forest dark, For the straight foreward pathway had been lost."
– Dante's *Inferno*

ONE

The rain pelted the windshield relentlessly.

Drops like little daggers assaulted the glass, only to be swept away by the frantic motion of the wipers. The scenery outside my window melted into dripping blobs of color through a screen of gray. I took my foot off the accelerator and slowed to forty miles an hour, focusing on the blurry yellow lines in the road.

Lightning stabbed the gray skies. A roar of thunder followed and the rain came down heavier, as if having been reprimanded for not falling hard enough.

"This rain is gonna keep on comin', folks," the radio meteorologist announced. Annoyed, I changed the station and resettled myself into my seat to the sound of Vivaldi's "Four Seasons, Summer." *Ha, Summer ...*

The rain morphed into hail. The visibility was slightly better, but now I was under a barrage of machine-gunned ice. I took a deep breath and tried to imagine myself on a sunny beach, sipping a strawberry margarita with a well-endowed man wearing nothing but a banana hammock and a smile.

In reality, I was as far from a cocktail on a sunny beach with Sven, the lust god, as possible. Nope, I was trapped in Colorado Springs in the middle of winter. If that weren't bad enough, I was late to work. To make matters worse? Today was not only my yearly review but I also had to give a presentation to the CEO, defending my decision to move forward with a risky and expensive marketing campaign. So, yes, being late didn't exactly figure into my plans.

With a sigh, I turned on my seat heater and tried to enact the presentation in my head, tried to remember the slides from my PowerPoint and each of the topics I needed to broach. I held my chin up high and cleared my throat, reminding myself to look the CEO and the board of directors in the eyes and not to say "um."

"Choc-o-late cake," I said out loud, opening my mouth wide and then bringing my teeth together again in an exaggerated way. "Choc-o-late cake." It was a good way to warm up my voice and to remind myself to pronounce every syllable of every word. And, perhaps the most important point to keep in mind—not to rush.

This whole being late thing wasn't exactly good timing, considering I was going to ask for a raise. With my heart rate increasing, I remembered the words of Jack Canfield, one of the many motivational speakers whose advice I followed like the Bible.

"'When you've figured out what you want to ask for,' Lily, 'do it with certainty, boldness and confidence,'" I quoted, taking a deep breath and holding it for a count of three before I released it for another count of three. "Certainty, boldness and confidence," I repeated to myself. "Choc-o-late cake."

Feeling my heart rate decreasing, I focused on counting the stacks of chicken coops in the truck ahead of me—five up and four across. Each coop was maybe a foot by a foot, barely enough room for the chickens to breathe. White feathers decorated the wire and contrasted against the bright blue of a plastic tarp that covered the top layer of coops. The tarp was held in place by a brown rope that wove in and around the coops like spaghetti. I couldn't help but feel guilty about the chicken salad sandwich currently residing in my lunch sack but then I remembered I had more important things to think about.

"Choc-o-late cake."

The truck's brake lights suddenly flashed red. The chicken coops rattled against one another as the truck lurched to a stop. A vindictive gust of wind caught the edge of the blue tarp and tore it halfway off the coops. As if heading for certain slaughter wasn't bad enough, the chickens now had to freeze en route. My concern for the birds was suddenly interrupted by another flash of the truck's brake lights.

Then I heard the sound of my cell phone ringing from my purse, which happened to be behind my seat. I reached behind myself, while still trying to pay attention to the road, and felt around for my purse. I only ended up ramming my hand into the cardboard box which held my velvet and brocade gown. The dress had taken me two months to make and was as historically accurate to the gothic period of the middle ages as was possible.

I finally reached my purse and then fingered my cell phone, pulling it out as I noticed Miranda's name on the caller ID.

"Hi," I said.

"I'm just calling to make sure you didn't forget your dress," Miranda said in her high pitch, nasally voice which sounded like a five-year-old with a cold.

"Forget it?" I scoffed, shaking my head at the very idea. "Are you kidding? This is only one of the most important evenings of our lives!" Yes, tonight would mark the night that, if successful, Miranda and I would be allowed to move up the hierarchical chain of our medieval reenactment club. We'd started as lowly peasants and had worked our way up to the merchant class and now we sought to be allowed entrance into the world of the knights.

"Can you imagine finally being able to enter the class of the knights?" Miranda continued. Even though I obviously couldn't see her, I could just imagine her pushing her Coke-bottle glasses back up to the bridge of her nose as she gazed longingly at the empire-waisted, fur trimmed gown (also historically accurate!) that I'd made for her birthday present.

"Yeah, instead of burlap, we can wear silk!" I chirped as I nodded and thought about how expensive it was going to be to costume ourselves if we actually did get admitted into the class of the knights.

"And maybe Albert will finally want to talk to me," Miranda continued, again in that dreamy voice.

I didn't think becoming a knight's lady would make Albert any more likely to talk to Miranda, but I didn't say anything. If the truth be told, Albert was far more interested in the knights than he ever was in their ladies.

"Okay, Miranda, I gotta go. I'm almost at work," I said and then heard the beep on the other line which meant someone else was trying to call me. I pulled the phone away from my ear and after quickly glancing at the road, I tried to answer my other call. That was when I heard the sound of brakes screeching.

I felt like I was swimming through the images that met me next—my phone landing on my lap as I dropped it, my hands gripping the wheel until my knuckles turned white, the pull of the car skidding on the slick asphalt, and the tail end of the truck in front of me, up close and personal. I braced myself for the inevitable impact.

Even though I had my seatbelt on, the jolt was immense. I was suddenly thrown forward only to be wrenched backwards again, as if by the invisible hands of some monstrous Titan. Tiny threads of anguish weaved up my spine until they became an aching symphony that spanned the back of my neck.

The sound of my windshield shattering pulled my thoughts from the pain. I opened my right eye—since the left appeared to be sealed shut—to find my face buried against the steering wheel.

I couldn't feel anything. The searing pain in my neck was soon a fading memory and nothing but the void of numbness reigned over the rest of my body. As if someone had turned on a switch in my ears, a sudden screeching met me like an enemy. The more I listened, the louder it got—a high-pitched wailing. It took me a second to realize it was the horn of my car.

My vision grew cloudy as I focused on the white of the feathers that danced through the air like winter fairies, only to land against the shattered windshield and drown in a deluge of red. Sunlight suddenly filtered through the car until it was so bright, I had to close my good eye.

And then there was nothing at all.

***

"Number three million, seven hundred fifty thousand forty-five."

I shook my head as I opened my eyes, blinking a few times as the scratchy voice droned in my ears. Not knowing where I was, or what was happening, I glanced around nervously, absorbing the nondescript beige of the walls. Plastic, multicolored chairs littered the room like discarded toys. What seemed like hundreds of people dotted the landscape of chairs in the stadium-sized room. Next to me, though, was only an old man. Glancing at me, he frowned. I fixed my attention on the snarly looking employees trapped inside multiple rows of cubicles. Choosing not to focus on them, I honed in on an electric board above me that read: *Number 3,750,045.*

The fluorescent green of the board flashed and twittered as if it had just zapped an unfortunate insect. I shook my head again, hoping to remember how the heck I'd gotten here. My last memory was in my car, driving in the rain as I chatted with Miranda. Then there was that truck with all the chickens. *An accident—I'd gotten into an accident.* After that, my thoughts blurred into each other. But nothing could explain why I was suddenly at the DMV.

Maybe I was dreaming. And it just happened to be the most lucid, real dream I'd ever had and the only time I'd ever realized I was dreaming while dreaming. *Hey, stranger things have happened, right?*

I glanced around again, taking in the low ceiling. There weren't any windows in the dreary room. Instead, posters with vibrant colors decorated the walls, looking like circus banners. The one closest to me read: *Smoking kills*. A picture of a skeleton in cowboy gear, atop an Appaloosa further emphasized the point. Someone had scribbled "ha ha" in the lower corner.

"Three million, seven hundred fifty thousand forty-five!"

Turning toward the voice, I realized it belonged to an old woman with orange hair, and 1950's-style rhinestone glasses on a string. A line of twelve or so porcelain cat statues, playing various instruments, decorated the ledge of her cubicle. What was it about old women and cats?

The cat lady scanned the room, peering over the ridiculous glasses and tapping her outlandishly long, red fingernails against the ledge. Her mouth was so tight, it swallowed her lips. As her narrowed gaze met mine, I flushed and averted my eyes to my lap, where I noticed a white piece of paper clutched in my right hand. I stared at the black numbers before the realization dawned on me.

Three million, seven hundred fifty thousand forty-five. She was calling my number! Without hesitation, I jumped up.

"That's me!" I announced, feeling embarrassed as the old man glared at me. "Sorry."

"Come on then," the woman interrupted. "I don't have all day."

Approaching her desk, I thought this dream couldn't get much weirder—I mean, I was number three million or something and yet there were only a few hundred people in the room? I handed the woman my ticket. She scowled at me, her scarlet lips so raw and wet that her mouth looked like a piece of talking sushi. She rolled the ticket into a little ball and flung it behind her. It landed squarely in her wastebasket, vanishing amid a sea of other white, scrunched paper balls.

"Name?" she asked as she worked a huge wad of pink gum between her clicking jaws.

"Um, Lily," I said with a pause, feigning interest in a cat playing a violin. It wore an obscene smile and appeared to be dancing, one chubby little leg lifted in the semblance of a jig. I touched the cold statue and ran the pad of my index finger along the ridges of his fur. I was beginning to think this might not be a dream, because I could clearly touch and feel things. But if this weren't a dream, how did I get here? It was like I'd just popped up out of nowhere.

"Last name?"

I faced the woman again. "Um, Harper."

The woman simply nodded, continuing to chomp on her gum like a cow chewing its cud. "Harper … Harper … Harper," she said as she stared at the computer screen in front of her.

"Um, could you, uh, tell me why I'm here?" My voice sounded weak and thin. I had to remind myself that I was the master of my own destiny and needed to act like it. And that was when I remembered my presentation. A feeling of complete panic overwhelmed me as I searched the wall for a clock so I could figure out how much time remained before I was due to sway a panel of mostly unenlightened penny-pinchers on why we needed to invest nearly a quarter of a million in advertising. "What time is it?" I demanded.

"Time?" the woman repeated and then frowned at me. "Not my concern."

I felt my eyebrows knot in the middle as I glanced behind me, wondering if there was a clock to be found anywhere. The blank of the walls was answer enough. I faced forward again, now more nervous than before and still at a complete loss as to where I was or why. "Um, what am I doing here?" I repeated, not meaning to sound so … stupid.

The woman's wrinkled mouth stretched into a smile, which looked even scarier than all the grimaces she'd given me earlier. She turned to the computer and typed something, her talon-like fingernails covering the keyboard with exaggerated flourishes. She hit "enter" and turned the screen to face me.

"You're here because you're dead."

"What?" It was all I could say as I felt the bottom of my stomach give way, my figurative guts spilling all over my feet. "You're joking."

She wasn't laughing though. Instead, she sighed like I was taking up too much of her time. She flicked her computer screen with the long, scarlet fingernail of her index finger. The tap against the screen reverberated through my head like the blade of a dull axe.

"Watch."

With my heart pounding in my chest, I glanced at the screen, and saw what looked like the opening of a low-budget film. Rain spattered the camera lens, making it difficult to decipher the scene beyond. One thing I could make out was the bumper-to-bumper traffic. It appeared to be a traffic cam in real time.

"I don't know what this has to do …"

She chomped louder, her jaw clicking with the effort, sounding like it was mere seconds from breaking. "Just watch it."

I crossed my arms against my flat chest and stared at the screen again. An old, Chevy truck came rumbling down the freeway, stopping and starting as the traffic dictated. The camera angle panned toward the back of the truck. I recognized the load of chicken coops piled atop one another. Like déjà vu, the camera lens zoomed in on the blue tarp covering the chickens. It was just a matter of time before the wind would yank the tarp up and over the coops, leaving the chickens exposed to the elements.

Realization stirred in my gut like acid reflux. I dropped my arms and leaned closer to the screen, still wishing this was a dream, but somehow knowing it wasn't. The camera was now leaving the rear of the truck and it started panning behind the truck, to a white Volvo S40. *My white Volvo*.

I braced myself against the idea that this could be happening—that I was about to see my car accident. Who the heck was filming? And moreover, where in the heck were they? This looked like it'd been filmed by more than one cameraman, with multiple angles, impossible for just one photographer.

I heard the sound of wheels squealing, knowing only too well what would happen next. I forced my attention back to the strange woman who was now curling her hair around her index finger, making the Cheeto-colored lock look edible.

"So someone videotaped my accident, what does that have to do with why I'm here?" I asked in an unsteady voice, afraid for her answer. "And you should also know that I'm incredibly late to work and I'm due to give a presentation not only to the CEO but also the board of directors."

She shook her head. "You really don't get it, do you?"

"I don't think *you* get it," I snapped. The woman grumbled something unintelligible and turned the computer monitor back towards her, then opened a manila file sitting on her desk. She rummaged through the papers until she found what she was looking for and started scanning the sheet, using her fingernail to guide her.

"Ah, no wonder," she said, snapping her wad of gum. She sighed as her triangular eyebrows reached for the ceiling. "He is not going to be happy."

I leaned on the counter, wishing I knew what was going on so I could get the heck out of here and on with my life. "No wonder what?"

She shook her head. "Not for me to explain. Gotta get the manager."

Picking up the phone, she punched in an extension, then turned around and spoke in a muffled tone. The fact that I wasn't privy to whatever she was discussing even though it involved me was annoying, to say the least. A few minutes later, she ended her cocooned conversation and pointed to the pastel chairs behind me.

"Have a seat. The manager will be with you in a minute."

"I don't have time for this," I said gruffly, trying to act out a charade of the fact that I *was* the master of my own destiny. "Didn't you hear me? I have to give a presentation!"

"The manager will be with you in a minute," she repeated in the same droll tone and then faced her screen again as if to say our conversation was over.

With hollow resignation, I threw my hands up in the air, but returned to the seat I'd hoped to vacate permanently. The plastic felt cold and unwelcoming. It creaked and groaned as if taunting me about my weight. I didn't need a stupid chair to remind me I was fat. I melted into the L-shaped seat and stretched my short legs out before me, trying to relax, and not to cry. I closed my eyes and breathed in for three seconds and out for three seconds.

Lily, stress is nothing more than a socially acceptable form of mental illness, I told myself, quoting one of my favorite self-help gurus, Richard Carlson. *And you aren't mentally ill, are you?*

No, but I might be dead! I railed back at myself. *But if you really were dead, why don't you feel like it?* I reached down to pinch myself, just to check if it would hurt and, what-do-you-know? It did … *So, really, I can't be dead. And furthermore, if I were dead, where in the heck am I now? I can't imagine the DMV exists anywhere near heaven. If I'd gone south instead … oh jeez …*

Don't be ridiculous, Lily Harper! This is nothing more than some sort of bad dream, courtesy of your subconscious because you're nervous about your presentation and your review.

I closed my eyes and willed myself to stop thinking about the what ifs. I wasn't dead. It was a joke. Heck, the woman was weird—anyone with musician cat statues couldn't be all there. And once I met with this manager of hers, I'd be sure to express my dissatisfaction.

You are the master of your own destiny, I told myself again.

I opened my eyes and watched the woman click her fingernails against the keyboard. The sound of a door opening caught my attention and I glanced up to find a very tall, thin man coming toward the orange-haired demon. He glanced at me, then headed toward the woman, who leaned in and whispered something in his ear. His eyes went wide; then his eyebrows knitted in the middle.

It didn't look good.

He nodded three, four times then cleared his throat, ran his hands down his suit jacket and approached me.

"Ms. Harper," he started and I raised my head. "Will you please come with me?"

I stood up and the chair underneath me sighed with relief. I ignored it and followed the man through the maze of cubicles into his office.

"Please have a seat," he said, peering down his long nose at me. He closed the door behind us, and in two brief strides, reached his desk and took a seat.

I didn't say anything, but sat across from him. He reached a long, spindly finger toward his business card holder and produced a white, nondescript card. It read:

Jason Streethorn

Manager

AfterLife Enterprises

"We need to make this quick," I started. "I'm late to work and I have to give a presentation. Can we discuss whatever damages you want to collect from the insurance companies of the other vehicles involved in the accident over the phone?" I paused for a second as I recalled the accident. "Actually, I think I was at fault."

"I see," he said and then sighed.

I didn't know what to say, so I just looked at him dumbly, ramming the sharp corners of the business card into the fleshy part of my index finger until it left a purple indentation in my skin.

The man cleared his throat. He looked like a skeleton.

"Ms. Harper, it seems we're in a bit of a pickle."

"A pickle?"

Jason Streethorn nodded and diverted his eyes. That's when I knew I wasn't going to like whatever came out of his mouth next. It's never good when people refuse to make eye contact with you.

"Yes, as I learned from my secretary, Hilda, you don't know why you're here."

"Right. And just so you know, Hilda wasn't very helpful," I said purposefully.

"Yes, she preferred I handle this."

"Handle this?" I repeated, my voice cracking. "What's going on?"

He nodded again and then took a deep breath. "Well, you see, Ms. Harper, you died in a car accident this afternoon. But the problem is: you weren't supposed to."

I was quiet for exactly four seconds. "Is this some sort of joke?" I sputtered finally while still trying to regain my composure.

He shook his head and glanced at me. "I'm afraid not."

His shoulders slumped as another deep sigh escaped his lips. He seemed defeated, more exhausted than sad. Even though my inner soul was starting to believe him—that didn't mean my intellect was prepared to accept it. Then something occurred to me and I glanced up at him, irritated.

"If I'm going to be on some stupid reality show, and this whole thing is a setup, you better tell me now because I've had enough," I said, scouring the small office for some telltale sign of A/V equipment. Or failing that, Ashton Kutcher. "And, furthermore, my boss and the board of directors aren't going to react well at all." I took a deep breath.

"Ms. Harper, I know you're confused, but I assure you, this isn't a joke." He paused and inhaled as deeply as I just had. "I'm sure this is hard for you to conceptualize. Usually, when it's a person's time to go, their guardian angel walks them through the process and accompanies them toward the light. Sometimes a relative or two might even attend." His voice trailed until the air swallowed it entirely.

Somehow, the last hour of my life, which made no sense, was now making sense. I guess dying was a confusing experience.

He jumped up, as if the proverbial lightbulb had gone off over his head. Then, throwing himself back into his chair, he spun around, faced his computer and began to type. Sighing, I glanced around, taking in his office for the first time.

Like the waiting room, there weren't any windows, just white walls without a mark on them. The air was still and although there wasn't anything offensive about the odor, it was stagnant, like it wouldn't know what to do if it met fresh air. The furniture consisted of Jason's desk, his chair and the two chairs across from him, one of which I occupied. All the furniture appeared to be made of cheap pine, like what you'd find at IKEA. Other than the nondescript furniture, there was a computer and beside that, a long, plastic tube about nine inches in diameter, that disappeared into the ceiling. It looked like some sort of suction device.

With a self-satisfied smile, he faced me again. "We have your whole life in our database."

He pointed toward the computer screen. "My whole life in his database" amounted to a word document with a humble blue border and my name scrawled across the top in Monotype Corsiva. It looked like a fifth grader's book report.

He eyed the document and moved his head from right to left with such vigor, he reminded me of a cartoon character eating corn. Then I realized he was scanning through the Lily Harper book report. With an enthusiastic nod, he turned toward me.

"Looks like you lost your first tooth at age six. Um … In school, you were a year younger than everyone else, but smarter than the majority of your class. You double majored in English and Political Science. You were a director of marketing for a prestigious bank."

"'Were' is a fitting word because after this, I'm sure I'll be fired," I grumbled.

The man paused, his eyes still on his computer. "When you were eighteen, you had a crush on your best friend and when you tried to kiss him, he pushed you away and told you he was gay."

I stood up so fast, my chair bucked. "Okay, I've heard enough."

The part about Matt rebuffing my kiss was something I'd never told anyone. I'd been too mortified. Guess the Word document was better than I thought.

"It's all there," Jason said as he turned to regard me with something that resembled sympathy.

"I don't understand …" I started.

He nodded, as though satisfied we'd moved beyond the "you're dead" conversation and into the "why you're dead" conversation. He pulled open his top desk drawer and produced a spongy stress ball—the kind you work in your palm. The ball flattened and popped back into shape under the tensile strength of his skeletal fingers.

"I'm afraid your guardian angel wasn't doing his job. This was supposed to be a minor accident—just to teach you not to text and drive, especially in the rain."

"I wasn't texting," I ground out.

Jason shrugged as if whatever I *was* doing was trivial and beside the point. "Unfortunately, your angel was MIA and now here you are."

I leaned forward, not quite believing my ears. "I have an angel?"

Jason nodded. "Everyone does. Some are just a little better than others."

I shook my head, wondering if there was a limit to how much information my small brain could process before it went on overload. "So, let me understand this, not only do I have a guardian angel, but mine isn't a very good one?"

"That about sums it up. Your angel …" He paused. "His name is Bill, by the way."

"Bill?"

"He's been on probation for … failing to do his duties for you and a few others."

My hands tightened on the arms of my chair as I wondered at what point my non-comprehending brain would simply implode with all this ridiculousness. "Probation?"

He nodded. "Yes, it seems he's had a bit of trouble with alcohol recently."

"My angel is an alcoholic?" I slouched into my

chair, the words "angel" and "alcoholic" swimming through the air as I began to doubt my sanity.

"Yes, I'm afraid so."

Jason parted his thin lips, but that exhausted look resurrected itself on his face. I was quick to interrupt, shock and anger suddenly warring within me until I couldn't contain them any longer. "This is the most ridiculous thing I've ever heard! Alcoholic angels? I didn't even know they could drink!"

"They can do everything humans can," he said in an affronted tone, like he was annoyed that I was annoyed.

I sat back into my chair, not feeling any better with the situation, but also figuring my outbursts were finished for the immediate future. Well, until I could come to terms with what was really going on. But flipping out wasn't going to do me any good. I needed to stay in control of myself and in control of my emotions. Wayne Dyer's words, "it makes no sense to worry about things you have no control over because there's nothing you can do about them," floated through my head as I tried to prepare myself for whatever I had coming.

Jason Streethorn, the office manager of death, folded his hands in his lap and leaned forward. "Since your angel, our employee, failed you, we do have an offer of restitution."

Apparently, this was where the business side of our conversation began. "Restitution?"

"Yes, because this oversight is our fault, I'd like to offer you the chance to live again."

I had to suspend my disbelief of being dead in the first place and just play along with him, figuring at some point I'd wake up and Jason Streethorn, the orange-haired woman and this DMV-like place would be nothing more than the aftermath of a cheese pizza and Coke eaten too close to bedtime. "Okay, that sounds good. What do I …"

He rebuffed me with his raised hand. "However, if you accept this offer, you'll have to be employed by AfterLife Enterprises."

I sank back into my chair, suddenly wanting nothing more than to pull my hair out. "What does that mean?"

He sighed, as though the explanation would take a while. "Unfortunately, AfterLife Enterprises is a bit on the unorganized side of late. When the computer system switched from 1999 to 2000, we weren't prepared, and a computer glitch resulted in thousands of souls getting misplaced."

The fact that death relied on a computer system which wasn't even as good as Windows XP was too much. "The Y2K bug didn't affect anyone."

Jason worked the stress ball between his emaciated fingers, making multiple knuckles crack, the sound imbedding itself in my psyche. "On Earth, it didn't affect anything, but such was not the case with the AfterLife." He exhaled like he was trying to expel all the air from his lungs. "Unfortunately, we were affected and it's a problem we've been trying to sort out ever since." He paused and shook his head like it was a great, big shame. Then he apparently remembered he had the recently dead to contend with and faced me again. "As I said before, due to this glitch, we've had souls sent to the Kingdom who should've gone to the Underground City. And vice versa." He paused. "And some souls are locked on the earthly plane as well. It's been a big nightmare, to say the least."

My mouth was still hanging open. "The Kingdom and the Underground City? Is that like heaven and hell?" Why did I have the sudden feeling he was going to start the Dungeons and Dragons lingo?

"Similar."

I rubbed my tired eyes and let it all sink in. So, not only were there bad dead people in heaven, aka the Kingdom, but there were good dead people in hell, aka the Underground City? And to make things even more complicated, there were bad and good dead people stuck on Earth?

"Is that still happening now? Or did you fix the computer glitch?" I asked, wondering if maybe I'd been sent to the wrong place. I thought this place seemed like hell from the get-go. And though I was never a church-goer, I definitely wasn't destined for the South Pole.

"We fixed the glitch, but that doesn't change the fact that there are still thousands of misplaced souls. And the longer those souls who should be in the Kingdom are left in the Underground City, or on the earthly plain, the bigger the chances of lawsuits against AfterLife Enterprises. We've already had a host of them and we can't afford anymore."

I didn't have the wherewithal to contemplate AfterLife lawsuits, so I focused on the other details. "So how are you going to get all those people, er souls, back where they belong?"

"That's where you would come in, should you accept this job offer."

"I would bring the spirits back?" I asked, aghast. "I'd be a ghost hunter or something?"

He laughed; it was the first time he seemed warm and, well, alive. Funny what a laugh will do for you.

"Yes, your title would be 'Retriever' and we have hundreds who, like you, are currently retrieving souls."

An image of the Ghostbusters jumped into my mind and I had to shake it free. Whatever this job entailed, I doubted it included slaying Slimer. "And if I don't agree?"

Jason shrugged and turned to the computer again. After a few clicks, he faced me with a frown. "Looks like you'll be on the waiting list for the Kingdom."

"The waiting list?" I asked, shocked. "I think I've led a pretty decent life!"

He shook his head and faced the computer again. "I show three accounts of thievery—when you were six, nine and eleven."

"I was just a kid!"

He cleared his throat and returned his attention to the Word doc. "I also show multiple accounts of cheating when you were in university."

Affronted, I launched myself from the chair. "I've never cheated in my life!"

He frowned, looking anything but amused. "No, but you aided a certain Jordan Summers by giving him the answers in your Biology class and I show that happened over the course of the semester."

I sat back down and folded my arms against my chest. "I would think helping someone wouldn't slate me for a waiting list!"

"Cheating takes more than one form." He glanced at the screen again. "Shall I go on?"

"No." I frowned. "So how long will I be on the waiting list?"

He leaned back in his chair and resumed working the stress ball. "You're fairly close to the top of the list since your offenses are only minor. I'd say about one hundred years."

"One hundred years!" I bit my lip to keep it from quivering. When I felt I could rationally conduct myself again, I faced Jason. "So where would I be for the next one hundred years?"

"In Shade."

I frowned. "And what is that? Like Limbo?"

"Yes, close to it."

"What would I do there?"

He shrugged. "Nothing, really. Shade exists merely as a loading dock for those who are awaiting the Kingdom … or the Underground City."

I didn't like the sound of that. "What's it like?"

"There is neither light nor dark, everything exists in gray. There's nothing good to look forward to, nor anything bad. You just exist."

"But if those people who are going to hell," I started.

"The Underground City," he corrected me. "Those destined for the Underground are kept separate from those destined for the Kingdom," he finished, answering my question before I even asked it.

I felt tears stinging my eyes. "Shade sounds like my idea of hell."

Jason shook his head while a wry chuckle escaped him. "Oh, no. The Underground City is much worse." He paused. "The good news is that if you do become a Retriever and you relocate ten souls, you can then go directly to the Kingdom and bypass Shade altogether."

"So I wouldn't have to go to Shade at all?"

"As long as you relocate ten souls, you bypass

Shade," he repeated, nodding as if to make it obvious that this was the choice I should make.

"What does retrieving these souls mean?"

He started rolling the stress ball against his desk. "We'd start you with one assignment, or one soul. With the help of a guide, you'd go after that soul and retrieve it." He paused. "Are you interested?"

I exhaled. Did I want to die and live the next century in Shade? The short answer was no. Did I want to be a soul-retriever? Not really, but I guessed it was better than dying.

"Okay, I guess so."

"We could start you out and see how you do. You can always decide not to do it."

"But then I'd die?"

"I'm afraid that's the alternative."

"Why can't you let me go back to my old life?"

He shook his head. "It's not possible. Your soul has already left your body. Once the soul departs, the body goes bad within three seconds. Unfortunately, you are way past your three seconds. That and the coroners have already pronounced you dead and the newspapers are preparing your obituary. Your mother was notified, as well."

Mom has been notified ... Something hollow and dreadful stirred in my gut and started climbing up my throat. I gulped it down, hell-bent on not getting hysterical. Tears welled up in my eyes and I

DOWNLOAD FREE E-BOOKS FROM HP MALLORY NOW!

Getting your FREE e-books is as easy as visiting:

www.hpmallory.com

Enter your email at the link at the top of the home page

Check your email!

~~~~

About H.P. Mallory:

H.P. Mallory is a New York Times and USA Today bestselling author. She writes paranormal fiction, heavy on the romance! H.P. lives in Southern California with her son and a cranky cat.

Printed in the USA
CPSIA information can be obtained
at www.ICGtesting.com
LVHW010734050424
776528LV00006B/99